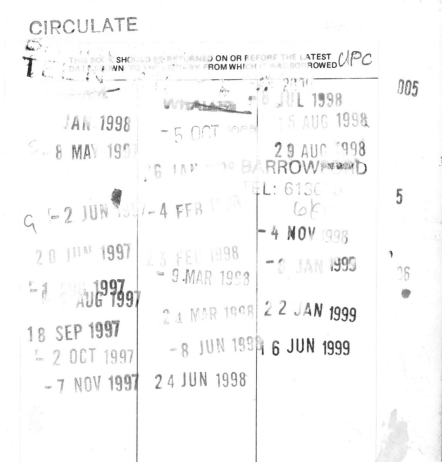

'Men are more trouble than they're worth. My mother told me that when I was seventeen; I didn't believe her then, but I sure as hell do now . . .'

Matilda Haycastle's love-affair with Luc Vander-auwera is going downhill, thanks to money problems, unemployment and a vicious divorce. Increasingly moody and difficult, Luc is away in Antwerp when his ten-year-old stepson Daniel has an accident, and Matilda is left to deal with the crisis on her own.

Rushing to the hospital armed with grapes and an Asterix book, she finds Daniel to be an endearing, if unusual child. But to her embarrassed horror, her visit is interrupted by the sudden arrival of the one woman she'd hoped never to meet – Daniel's ruthless, unpleasant mother Marie-Paule, currently divorcing Luc for adultery with Matilda.

Undeterred, Matilda visits Daniel again, to find he has been removed from hospital against his doctor's advice. Going to Marie-Paule's house to see the child, Matilda and Daniel's doctor instead discover the young woman's murdered corpse. Luc, clearly hiding something, is soon top of the list of suspects.

Determined to discover the truth, Matilda sets about investigating the secrets of Marie-Paule's complex and shadowy past. And when Daniel asks her to find out who his real father is, the case becomes even more complicated . . .

By the same author:

DREADFUL LIES

The Cuckoo Case

Michèle Bailey

MACMILLAN

First published 1995 by Macmillan London

an imprint of Macmillan General Books
Cavaye Place London SW10 9PG
and Basingstoke

Associated companies throughout the world

ISBN 0 333 61937 4

9 8 7 6 5 4 3 2 1

A CIP catalogue record for this book is available from
the British Library

Phototypeset by Intype, London
Printed by Mackays of Chatham PLC, Chatham, Kent

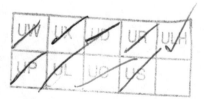

Chapter One

Men are more trouble than they're worth. My mother told me that when I was seventeen; I didn't believe her then, but I sure as hell do now.

What I can't understand is why the same damn thing keeps happening: red-hot passion the first few months, then gradual creeping disillusionment. What looks like a dead cert to start with rapidly becomes a never-wozzer once gritty reality hits. I expect it's my own fault; my selection procedures probably need reviewing.

Admittedly, reality had been particularly gritty since ex-Inspector Luc Vanderauwera and I had become, as they say, an item. After ten years in the police force, he was suddenly unemployed, and jobs were thin on the ground. Brown stuff was still falling on our heads from the murder which had thrown us together.* His divorce had turned vicious. Money problems were pressing. He was bored, moody and broke. I was tired, stressed-out, and less than overjoyed at being co-respondent in the aforementioned divorce.

It was all part of a general disorientation. Even safe old Belgium seemed about to split into its component parts; everybody had a bad attack of federalism. And it had been cold in Brussels, that winter. To cap it all, my cat Hortense had started ripping up the apartment. But she was the only one of us acting normally.

* *Dreadful Lies* (Macmillan 1994)

1

Then there was that phone call. Worthy of Samuel Beckett, it was, though that wasn't what sprang to mind at the time. The voice was that of a worried middle-aged woman, speaking French. She asked if Luc was there. I said he wasn't. There was a lengthy pause. Did I know where he was? He was in Antwerp, I said. There was another lengthy pause.

'Oh, dear,' she said desolately, 'I don't know what to do.'

One of my ancestors must have been an agony aunt. I shifted the phone to the other hand and sat down.

'Tell me about it,' I invited.

There was another long pause. Then she said uncertainly, 'Well, who are you?'

'My name's Matilda Haycastle. I'm a close friend of Mr Vanderauwera.'

That's one way of putting it, anyway.

'Oh, I see,' she said, in the way people have, when they don't see at all. 'Well, maybe you can help. This is the Clinique St Michel. It's Daniel, Mr Vanderauwera's son. He's had an accident at school and he's here at the hospital and we can't contact his mother or his grandparents. The poor little mite's been here for hours and nobody's even been to see him.' She sounded as distressed as if it were her own son.

'Is he badly hurt?' I asked, alarmed.

'Oh no, no, just cuts and bruises and concussion. He fell off the roof of the bicycle shed. I don't know what the teachers thought they were doing. You'd think an expensive school like that would supervise the children better, wouldn't you?'

'Listen—' I broke in before she could get onto the iniquities of the Belgian private education system. 'Tell Daniel I'll be right over to see him. I'll try and get a message to his father. And you keep on trying his mother and grandparents. Someone's bound to answer sooner or later.'

My brisk tone had the desired effect. She thanked me and rang off.

It was a wet weekday afternoon in early March. Why wasn't I at work, you wish to know? Well, to tell the truth, temp work was a bit thin on the ground right then; the recession had hit us at last. I'd only had a couple of weeks' work since Christmas. Liquidity problems were looming on my horizon too. I looked at Hortense, who was lying on her back under the radiator, eyes closed and paws in the air, and reflected on life's essential unfairness for a moment. Then I got busy.

Luc was doing a few days' casual work up in Flanders and I had to admit to myself that his absence was something of a relief. He hadn't left a contact number in Antwerp, so I called the house he shared with a friend and left a message on the answering machine. I muffed it. I usually do, because I hate answering machines. Then I set off for the hospital.

I'd only met Daniel twice, briefly. He was a reserved child of ten. He wasn't really Luc's son. He was the result of some hanky-panky between Luc's wife Marie-Paule and a chap called Olivier Delfosse. He didn't seem to have much of a life, with no real father and a mother who, from all accounts, would have taken first prize in the Royal Dairy Show. I'm not particularly fond of kids, but it seemed like a rum deal to me. So I stopped off on the way to buy a kilo of grapes and a comic strip for the patient.

Astérix was probably about the right level, I thought. The endless rows of *Bandes Dessinées*, or BDs, as comic strips are universally known in Belgium, ran the gamut from kids' cartoons right through science-fiction, westerns, detective stories, adventure and historical up to the really adult stuff on the very top shelf. I cast a quick glance along the racks, grabbed the first Astérix that came to hand, paid for it, and dashed back to the car, which was holding up a line of irritated traffic. This city's getting impossible to move around in. Too many damned cars, that's the problem. I realized I was frowning and tried to stop before the wind changed.

The dragon at the hospital reception told me where to go. I emerged from the lift at the correct floor and asked the girl at the desk where Daniel Vanderauwera was. A man in a white coat looked up from the clipboard he was reading, gave me an abrupt once-over, and said in a brusque voice, 'I don't know what's kept you, Madame Vanderauwera, but your child has been here for four hours already. Permit me to say that perhaps you should think about reorganizing your priorities.'

He was about forty-five, not over-tall, and untidily dressed under the open white coat. He looked intelligent, angry and very tired; his square face was deeply lined. His hair was thick and grizzled and hadn't seen a comb since early that morning. He looked like the kind of man who smoked a pipe. His expression was definitely unfriendly.

I stood there staring stupidly, clutching my grapes and my comic book, and said the first thing I could think of, which was, unoriginally, 'But I'm not Daniel's mother.'

He stared back for a moment, then said, equally abruptly, 'Well, who are you, then?'

'A friend of Daniel's father. The hospital rang me, so I said I'd come.'

There was a moment's pause. The girl at the desk had gone into hiding behind her high parapet. Then my attacker groaned, lifted a hand to his face and rubbed his nose tiredly.

'I'm sorry,' he said, with grim ruefulness. 'It's been a long day. I apologize. I apologize. That'll teach me to shoot my mouth off.'

He looked so comical that I relaxed and laughed.

'Don't worry about it,' I said. 'I'm difficult to offend. Are you Daniel's doctor? How is he?'

'He's fine. Yes. I'm Marius Charpentier.'

4

'Matilda Haycastle,' I said, juggling my parcels and offering a hand. He took it in a very strong, warm grasp.

'Are you English?' he asked.

'English father, French mother.'

'Ah, the answer to my prayers. May I practise on you?'

'It depends what you mean.'

'Conversation,' he said, and laughed. It took ten years off him. I liked him.

'Daniel's through here,' he said. 'It's good of you to come. Nobody else seems much interested.'

It was a small private room, containing one bed with a thin fair-haired child in it. Daniel had been drawing; some sheets of paper lay scattered on the bed. He looked up as we entered, then like a well-mannered child he carefully gathered up the papers, put them aside, and looked up at us obediently.

'Daniel, here's a pretty lady to see you,' said Marius Charpentier, somewhat to my surprise.

'*Bonjour*, Mathilde,' Daniel turned his cheek up to be kissed. I obliged.

'Hello, Daniel,' I said. 'What have you been up to?'

'I fell off the roof,' he said, as I sat down. His eyes were on the Astérix book.

'I'll leave you together,' said Marius Charpentier, and did.

'I brought you a book. And some grapes. I hope you like grapes. If not, I'll eat them.'

'Oh, no, I like grapes.' Daniel paused and eyed me speculatively. 'I like chewing them up and spitting the pips out.'

'Well, there's a funny thing,' I said, unpacking the parcel, 'so do I. I'll get the waste-paper basket.'

He didn't seem to be any the worse for the accident, apart from a bruise or two. We ate the grapes, spat the pips out, most of them into the waste-bin, and read the Astérix book together aloud. Daniel grew animated at the adventures of the little Gaulish warrior among the

5

Britons. He was good at the funny voices. It was the most relaxing hour I'd spent in a month of Sundays. In fact we were having such a good time, I forgot how late it was and was brought up sharp when the door suddenly opened and a woman walked into the room.

I knew who she was immediately, though I'd never met her before. I'd hoped rather forlornly that I never would.

She was a tall golden blonde in her late thirties. Ten years ago she must have been gorgeous. Now there was a little too much flesh under her jaw and round the middle of her body, though she carried herself regally. It was a lioness's face, strong-boned, straight-nosed, wide-mouthed, the beauty of it marred by a permanent frown between the eyebrows and strongly marked lines of discontent around the mouth. She wore a great deal of make-up, as is the habit of Belgian women of the moneyed classes, and her long, thick hair was combed up and back, falling to her shoulders. She was wearing a full-length coat in soft grey fur over a silk suit with a pleated skirt. She had long, beautiful legs. She looked like a woman who knew exactly what she wanted and let nothing stop her from getting it.

I must say that if I'd had to choose the last situation in the world I wanted to be in, this was probably it. She was divorcing her husband for adultery with me. Awkward, to say the least. No, I'll go further; the potential for unpleasantness was vast.

Fortunately, we weren't alone. Daniel was there. Also, Marie-Paule was followed into the room by a tall dark man with a camel-coloured overcoat thrown over his well-cut business suit. He had a large pleasant face with the blue beginnings of a five o'clock shadow, and was wearing an exclusive men's cologne of a well-known brand which I particularly dislike, having once gone several rounds with a would-be Casanova drenched in the stuff. He carried a large gift-wrapped parcel under his arm. I was just hazarding a wild guess as to his identity when Daniel said politely: '*Bonjour*, Maman. *Bonjour*, Oncle Olivier.'

Marie-Paule's fierce hazel eyes swept right over me as if I didn't exist and came to rest on her son. Her face softened; she stroked the silver-fair hair with a surprisingly gentle gesture and bent to kiss the proffered cheek. Olivier Delfosse, casting a rather apologetic glance at me, came forward eagerly with the gift held out.

'*Bonjour, fiston*,' he said. 'I brought you this.'

'Oh, thank you,' Daniel said in that polite little voice. He took the gift and laid it on the bed, showing no signs of wanting to open it. 'Mathilde came to see me,' he added.

It was time I wasn't there. I got up and said, 'I'll be off now, Daniel. I hope you feel better soon.'

He reached up and caught my hand. 'Will you come and see me again?' he asked.

'I don't think that'll be necessary, Daniel,' his mother broke in. 'You won't be here very long.'

She picked up the comic strip and turned to face me. We were of a height, eye-to-eye for the first time. The expression on her face was one of icy contempt.

'Please take this with you,' she said, holding the book out to me. 'I don't care for my son reading this kind of thing.'

For a moment I felt like chucking it in her face, but that would have been childish, wouldn't it? So I gave her glare for glare, then took the book and left without a word. But out in the corridor I stopped, hot with anger. For two pins I'd have gone back and poked her in the nose. Behind me, someone said my name. It was Marius Charpentier.

'From your face, I'd say you got the same treatment I did,' he observed.

'She gave me the book back,' I said, still feeling hot.

'Give it to me. I'll see Daniel gets it when she's gone.'

I handed it to him, and was shocked to find my fingers

7

were trembling. He noticed and gave me a sharp glance.

'Your nerves are bad,' he said. 'Tell me something. What is it with this family? Daniel told me that his father isn't really his father at all.'

'Daniel knows?' I asked, startled. That was news to me.

'Apparently,' Marius Charpentier said. 'Would you care to let me in on it? There's a nice little room here where we can sit down.'

There was. We sat. I said, 'Marie-Paule tricked Luc into marrying her by saying she was pregnant, but in fact it was Olivier who was the father.'

'The chap who's in there with her now?' Marius Charpentier said, still frowning.

I nodded.

'So that explains why your friend's an absentee father. How long has he known?'

'Since Daniel was two or three.'

'Did he take steps to renounce paternity?'

I shook my head.

'So legally, he retains all his responsibilities?'

'I suppose so.'

'Well, then, he should assume them,' Marius Charpentier said trenchantly.

'He's not a particularly paternal man,' I said carefully. 'And he says he doesn't have anything in common with Daniel.'

'That's all very well, but what about the child? He told me he doesn't want Oncle Olivier to be his father. I take it there's a divorce on the horizon?'

'Several,' I said glumly, and sat back with a sigh.

'What about a cup of tea?' said the abrupt man by my side.

It was a welcome thought. He fetched the tea from a machine in the corridor. The best that could be said for it was that it was hot and wet. We sat in silence for a moment, sipping. Then Marius Charpentier said, 'Is she planning to marry this Olivier?'

'I don't know. It's a bit like snakes and ladders. Marie-Paule's divorcing Luc for adultery with me and he's divorcing her for adultery with Olivier. The trouble is that Olivier's married too, so he and his wife would have to get divorced before he and Marie-Paule could get married.'

'And what about you and your friend?'

I looked down at my plastic cup. 'The question hasn't arisen.'

He didn't pursue that particular rabbit, which was a relief. Instead he said, 'What a mess,' and I had to agree. A second later a nurse rushed in looking for him and he had to abandon both the tea and me. I went home thoughtfully.

Luc was due back late Friday night. He usually spent the weekend with me, but this time we'd made no definite arrangements, which was annoying because I had no idea when he'd turn up. But I hadn't the slightest intention of waiting in like a dutiful Victorian maiden, so on Saturday morning I left a note Sellotaped to the downstairs doorbell and went about my usual business. It was just as well I did: the note was still there when I came back in the late afternoon. About half an hour later, the familiar double-ring sounded and Luc came up.

He was looking enormously pleased with himself. He had a new black leather jacket on. Isn't it funny how policemen, even ex-policemen, seem to have such a penchant for black leather? It made him look like a handsome fascist. It also looked expensive.

'Wow! Nice,' I said. 'Did you rob a bank?'

For some reason, the crack fell flat. The pleased look faded perceptibly. Then Luc said, 'This driving work pays well. I'm in funds. I'll take you out to dinner.'

He threw the jacket across the back of the sofa and came over to kiss me. Hortense sniffed at the jacket, then settled down on it, tramping and purring. I went to make coffee.

'Did you get all the messages about Daniel?' I called back into the living-room.

There was a short silence, then Luc said: 'I could hardly fail to. The whole world seems to have been looking for me. I went to the hospital this morning. They didn't really need me. Daniel's fine. He'll be out early next week.'

'I went over on Thursday,' I said, coming back with the coffee.

'It was good of you, but you needn't have bothered,' he said casually, stroking Hortense under the chin.

'Well, somebody had to,' I said, and then winced, because it sounded like a reproach. Luc's face tightened.

'Don't you give me a lecture too,' he said shortly. 'I've already had one from the doctor at the hospital. Bloody cheek.'

Despite myself I had to smile. It was in Marius Charpentier's nature to have a go. A born crusader. Luc wasn't looking at me.

'Well, do you want to go out or don't you?' he said, still stroking Hortense.

I've had less enthusiastic invitations, but I don't remember when.

We went out, but it was an edgy meal. Luc was unusually tight-mouthed and I had to make all the running. In the end I lapsed into defeated silence, which doesn't happen very often. I started to fidget like a schoolkid and was hugely relieved when the waiter finally brought the bill. Luc looked round for his jacket, which was hanging on a hook near my head.

'Pass my wallet, will you?' he said. 'The inside pocket.'

'A pickpocket's delight,' I said, getting up. 'And you an ex-policeman,' and then I stopped, because in my hand was not only Luc's wallet, but, tucked between the two halves of it, his passport.

I hardly had time to register more than an impression because Luc, in one fast movement, leaned across the

10

table and whisked both items out of my hands. Without comment, he opened the wallet and started to count out thousand-franc notes. I looked at the bent brown head and said, 'You need a passport to go to Antwerp these days?'

No answer.

I'm the persistent sort.

'Don't tell me,' I said, 'Flanders has declared itself independent and seceded from the European Community?'

'Matilda, give the detective work a rest,' Luc said curtly. 'So I've got my passport with me. No big deal. Let's go home.'

Well, maybe there was nothing in it, after all. But it was odd, all the same. You don't need a passport to travel inside the Community these days, nor even to Scandinavia; an ID card alone is sufficient. And why snatch it out of my hand as if it were on fire?

Things didn't get any better at home. We went to bed, but even that wasn't the same these days. I caught myself lying there wondering if I'd taken the meat out of the freezer for tomorrow; if ever there was a sure sign that a love affair's going down the tubes, that's it. Then I couldn't sleep. Luc was well away, so I crept out of bed and went to play games with the computer for an hour or two. Hortense climbed on my lap and from there onto the keyboard. She likes to try and catch the little men on the screen.

'What would you do, H?' I asked, stroking her. A pointless question, because being an apartment cat, Hortense has never even met a cat of the opposite sex and in any case she's been what my vet calls 'neutralized'. I stared glumly at the computer screen. This state of affairs couldn't go on. It was getting painful. Someone was obviously going to have to be the executioner and it looked like it was going to be me.

Chapter Two

Sunday the seventh of March was a day to remember. The phone woke us up at 11.30. A man's voice asked for Luc. As I trailed yawning into the kitchen, I heard him speaking Flemish low and fast and urgent. I stopped what I was doing to listen. I couldn't understand most of it, but I got the last sentence all right. It was, 'Don't ever call me here again,' followed by the sound of the receiver slamming down. Luc appeared in the kitchen doorway.

'I have to go out,' he said. 'Can I borrow the car for a few hours?'

'But we're going to the cinema,' I protested.

'I can't,' he said. 'Can I have the car? If not, I'll call a taxi.'

'Where are you going?'

'I haven't got time to answer questions,' he said curtly. 'Can I have the car?'

I got my bag and gave him the car keys silently, then sat in the kitchen with my cup of coffee while he dressed and went out, which he did without another word. That's it, I told myself. I don't have to put up with this. Let him sort out his own problems. I've had enough.

My mother chose that day for her periodic call to check if I'm still alive. She's never approved of my involvement with a penniless Flemish ex-cop. My mother has always hoped I'd marry a Frenchman with a luxury apartment in the *seizième* and a modest but exquisite château within weekending distance of Paris. I've always

12

been a disappointment to my mother. It was quite an exercise not to let her get a sniff of what was going on, but I think I managed it. By the time I put the phone down, I was sweating with the effort of so much diplomacy. I glanced at my watch; it was two o'clock.

Any hopes of doing something with the afternoon were shattered when my *concierge* and her husband appeared to take the temperature of all my radiators. There seemed to be something wrong with the heating system in the building. I made inconsequential conversation for twenty minutes while Monsieur tapped and drained and twiddled. By the time they disappeared, it was past three. No sign of Luc. To hell with Luc, I thought. I'm going to visit Daniel again.

On the bus, half-way to the hospital, I suddenly thought: suppose Marie-Paule's there? Then I thought: I can always hide in Doctor Charpentier's little room till she's gone. But in the event, I needn't have worried; she wasn't there.

Neither was Daniel.

I stood looking at the empty room, ridiculously disappointed. Then as I turned to go, I heard a voice I recognized and saw Marius Charpentier approaching. He was in civvies; his pullover was vintage Marks and Sparks with a small hole right in the front where the wool had worn away.

'Your sweater needs mending,' I said.

An expression of delight came over his face. 'Are you volunteering?' he asked. 'Daniel's gone home. Maman brought in her own paediatrician and I was overruled. I have something to show you.'

From behind the reception desk, he took a transparent folder with a few sheets of paper in it, and fanned them out for me to see. They were simple pencil-drawings of people. They weren't in any sense elaborate or technically brilliant, but with a few strokes, the artist had succeeded in capturing the essence of his originals. I had no difficulty in recognizing a portrait of Marius Charpentier, and, with a sudden gasp of amazement, myself.

'Daniel did these?' I exclaimed, and Marius Charpentier nodded, his eyes twinkling.

'The nurses found them under the mattress when they made up the bed. Remarkable, aren't they? An astonishing talent.'

'But he's only ten!' I said.

'It's something you're born with, like an ear for music.'

'What are you going to do with these?'

'Return them to Daniel,' he said. 'I thought I'd go this afternoon. My shift's just ended.'

I had another comic book under my arm, which I'd hoped to smuggle in to Daniel.

'If you're going over, will you take this too?' I asked.

'Why don't you come with me?' he said, looking at me challengingly. 'I'm sure Daniel would be very happy to see you again.'

'What about Maman?'

'To hell with Maman. She can't have everything her own way. Let's go and annoy her.'

His air of defiance was comical and infectious. I had to laugh. 'You're on,' I said. 'I don't have my car with me. I came by bus.'

'Not to worry,' he said. 'I'm parked underground. I'll just get my coat.'

His car was a small white van of the type that French farmers habitually drive: of a basic standard of comfort and with room for a couple of sheep in the back. It was a vehicle of some antiquity. I studied it carefully.

'Where's the key?' I asked.

English humour doesn't always translate well. Marius Charpentier looked at me blankly.

'To wind it up,' I explained, making a circular motion with my hand.

He said nothing, clamped a tweed hat onto his head, and opened the door for me. A large no-smoking sign

14

was pasted on the dashboard. So much for my theory about the pipe. The back of the car bore a World Wildlife sticker, an Amnesty International sticker and a *Médecins Sans Frontières* sticker. The mess inside was fascinating and varied – it included a football, a couple of tins of cat food, medical journals in various languages, a vegetarian cookbook, a torch, an ancient umbrella, a new pair of gardening gloves, a ball of green twine and a pair of large, muddy football boots. In the words of the old French proverb, a cow couldn't have found her calf in there.

It was cold inside. I shivered and pulled my anorak collar up.

'You should wear a hat,' Marius said, fumbling with the keys.

'They don't make cars tall enough,' I replied. My head just about grazed the roof as it was, and my knees were in my chest. The disadvantages of being tall.

'Did you know that most of your body heat escapes out of the top of your head?' he pursued.

The engine coughed and burst into life.

He drove like a French farmer too: at a leisurely pace in the middle of the road. It was a refreshing change in a town where driving sends the stress-levels off the top of the scale. He took his time and didn't get flustered. I decided to change my driving habits forthwith and add a few extra years to my life.

'We had an exciting day yesterday,' he remarked, glancing sideways at me. 'Your friend came in to see Daniel.'

'I know. I gather you had words.'

'He doesn't like taking advice, does he?'

'No,' I said carefully. That was the understatement of the millenium. I saw him glance at me again in his sharp way. He went on, 'And then he had a stand-up fight with his wife. I take it she still is his wife?'

'A fight?' I echoed, unbelieving.

'They nearly came to blows. The whole floor had ring-

15.

side seats. Most edifying. Just what we needed to wake us all up.'

'Oh, God,' I said, with a groan. 'Who won?'

'I think, on balance, she came out on top. After all, she had the moral high ground, considering she got to Daniel's bedside before he did, even if only fractionally. That Olivier chap was there too, but he had the good sense to stay out of it.'

'I think I'm going to leave the country,' I said glumly. 'I've had about as much of the Vanderauweras as I can take.'

'Surely there's a less radical solution?' he said, and I suddenly wondered how much I was giving away.

Marie-Paule lived in a beautiful town house on the Avenue Molière. I wondered how on earth she could afford such a pricey location. Mummy and Daddy, probably. Marius parked in front of a garage.

'You'll get towed away,' I said.

He smiled, reached into the back, hauled out a cardboard sign and propped it in the front window. It said, *'Médecin en visite d'urgence'*. He winked at me.

'Never fails,' he said.

A small flight of stone steps with a gracious wrought-iron balustrade led up to Marie-Paule's front door. Marius marched straight up defiantly and rang the doorbell loud and long. We waited.

I should have expected that Marie-Paule would have a maid. The door flew open to reveal a distraught middle-aged woman still in outdoor clothes. Her dark-blue coat was half-unbuttoned, with a scarf hanging from one shoulder, and her crocheted woollen hat was at a wild angle. She was hysterical and Spanish. I couldn't make head or tail of the flood of anguished words pouring out of her mouth, except for one, and that only because she kept repeating it over and over again.

'*Muerta, muerta, muerta!*'

Chapter Three

Marie-Paule was dead all right. She was lying bang in the middle of the sitting-room carpet, flat on her back, in an expensive silk kimono which was covered in blood. One slipper had fallen off. Her eyes were wide open. I stood at a safe distance, my arm round the maid, who was sobbing quietly now, while Marius made a quick examination. He looked up at me and said, 'One shot, just in the right place. Several hours ago, I'd say. You haven't seen a dead body before?'

I hadn't seen a dead body before. I said 'No' with difficulty.

'I wish I could say the same,' Marius said grimly. He stood up and asked the maid, in extremely competent Spanish, for the telephone.

'Don't touch anything,' he said. 'We'll go in the hall. There's nothing I can do for her now.'

He'd closed the staring eyes, which helped somewhat. I dredged up the remnants of my Spanish O level and asked the maid where Daniel was. It seemed he'd gone straight to his grandparents' house on coming out of hospital. He usually spent Sunday with them, she said. Sunday was her day off too. She'd just got back, walked in, and found Marie-Paule dead on the carpet. Then we'd rung the doorbell. She was beginning to get over the shock now, so Marius sent her off to make a cup of tea while we waited for the police.

They were very quick. Of course, they would be.

17

Marie-Paule's father had been a high-ranking policeman – this was a family affair. I sat in the hall on a Louis Quinze chair, next to the maid, Consuela, a plain woman of middle height and size. I lost count of the number of people who came in. Marius knew the *médecin-légiste*, a sharp-looking dark woman in horn-rimmed glasses, and immediately went into a huddle with her before disappearing into the living-room. People came and went. Consuela was taken off into another room, looking very scared. A large man in a shabby suit approached me and I prepared myself for the inevitable 'few questions'.

Marius had obviously already briefed them. I was grateful for that, because my brain seemed to be grid-locked. I confirmed his information, adding that I'd only met Marie-Paule once before, though I knew Daniel a little better, as I was a close friend of his father. I gave them Luc's address and phone number. As I did so, the door opened to admit a tall, very upright elderly man with a distinguished face and grey hair. Around me, everyone fell embarrassedly silent as people do in the presence of the bereaved. Marie-Paule's father. He gave one glance round, nodded in a dignified manner, and went through into the living-room without a word. Around me, the activity resumed, a little muted.

The living-room door opened again and Marius emerged frowning, his hair standing on end. He came straight over to me.

'They want us all to go down to the police station,' he said. 'I'm afraid we're in for a long night. You and Consuela have to go in the police car. I'm being allowed to drive myself down. Are you OK?'

'Fine,' I said, which was something of an exaggeration.

There was a crowd of gawpers outside, no doubt avidly hoping to catch a glimpse of the body. Half-way to the police station, my brain suddenly switched on again. I sat there staring at the back of the driver's neck, my eyes wide open like an electrocuted cat. Luc! No wonder they wanted to find him. I remembered him telling me himself once that ninety-nine murders out of a hundred are committed by a close relative, usually a spouse. I had a wild impulse to leap out of the car and rush to warn him. But surely, surely it couldn't have been him? My treacherous memory obligingly furnished me with almost every unfavourable remark Luc had ever made about Marie-Paule, some of which were pretty virulent. But surely everybody says at least once in their life: 'I could break that bitch's neck.'

Don't they?

It was six o'clock when we got to the police station. Two hours later I was still sitting in front of a bare desk waiting to be interviewed. My particulars had been taken, as had my fingerprints. I had been treated politely and offered a cup of coffee. I wanted to go home. I was dying to know what was going on. I made a mental vow not to use the expression 'dying' ever again.

At half-past eight the door suddenly opened and two men came in. The elder, a tall, amiable-looking person in a nondescript suit, shook my hand, saying, 'I'm so sorry to have kept you waiting, Mademoiselle Haycastle. It is "Mademoiselle", isn't it?'

I don't know what the hell that had to do with anything. He waved an inviting hand at the chair I had just vacated, and seated himself behind the desk. A pair of indeterminate-coloured eyes twinkled in a long brown face topped by thinning hair. He looked like a vicar in an English drawing-room comedy.

'I'm Claude Roland,' he said. 'Commissaire in charge of the investigation. This is Inspector Lebrun. Doctor Charpentier has given a very full account of how you discovered the body, but I'd like to hear it in your own words. By the way, how well did you know Madame Vanderauwera?'

'Scarcely at all,' I said. 'I met her once, at the hospital last week.'

'But you're the co-respondent in her divorce case?' the other man said.

I turned to survey him.

He had perched himself on the window-sill at the side of the room, legs stretched out, ankles crossed and arms folded. He was in his mid-twenties, with slicked-back dark hair and round, gold-rimmed glasses. The white shirt was expensive and spotless, the cuff-links gold, the tie a Dior original – this wasn't your average copper-on-the-beat at all. He looked insufferably pleased with himself. I took an instant dislike to him. I stared at him coldly for a minute and said, 'That hardly makes us related.'

'Did you like her?' Roland said.

They were a double-act. Morecambe and Wise.

'Not exactly,' I said, turning back. 'She wasn't what you might call polite.'

'Did you expect her to be?' the younger man said.

I declined to comment.

Roland said, 'So what happened this afternoon?'

I told him, in my own words. He nodded.

'I see. I see. By the way, how did you spend the rest of the day?'

'I was at home,' I said.

'Can you prove it?' the young man said, needling.

I decided not to bother to turn round this time.

'Luc – Mr Vanderauwera left at about midday,' I said to Roland. 'And then my mother called me from England. And the *concierge* and her husband came in to do something to the heating system.'

'What time was that?' Roland said. He took a gold fountain-pen out of his inside pocket, uncapped it, took a block of squared paper out of a drawer, and started to write. The technological revolution has passed some of us by.

'My mother called around one-thirty. She was on the phone for some time. The *concierges* appeared just after that. They were there for about half an hour. I left the apartment around three-thirty to go to the clinic.'

'And you said Mr Vanderauwera left at midday. Where was he going?'

'I don't know,' I said. 'There was a phone call which woke us up and he got dressed and left straight away.'

'What was the phone call about?'

'I don't know,' I said again. Despite myself, I could hear defensiveness in my voice. 'It was in Flemish and I don't understand Flemish too well. And I was in the kitchen.'

'And the phone is . . .?'

'In the hall.'

'I see,' said Roland again.

'And you're sure he didn't tell you where he was going?' the young man said.

'Positive.'

'Isn't that unusual?'

'Not recently,' I said before I could stop myself, and felt myself flushing. There was a small pause; I could feel them digesting this statement.

'Perhaps you can enlighten us on one or two small details?' Roland resumed, re-capping his fountain-pen. 'Initially, Monsieur and Madame Vanderauwera filed for divorce by mutual consent. Then Madame changed her mind and sued on the grounds of adultery. Do you have any idea why?'

'Revenge,' I said.

'And then her husband made a counter-accusation, naming Mr Delfosse? Was there much bad feeling between her and her husband?'

I saw the pit yawn, but there wasn't much I could say except the truth. 'About as much as there is between any divorcing couple,' I said.

'Do you speak from experience?' the young man said, rather derisively.

Little squirt. I ignored him.

21

'Did you know that Madame Vanderauwera had stated her intention of taking her husband to the cleaners?' Roland said gently.

'I assumed that was the case. It usually is, in Belgium. Luc hasn't discussed the details with me.'

'And Mr Vanderauwera is currently unemployed, and his financial situation is somewhat shaky?'

I suddenly remembered the new leather jacket and the expensive meal.

'Yes?' Roland said, watching my face closely.

'I really don't know what his financial situation is,' I said, uncomfortably. 'There aren't many jobs going for somebody with his qualifications.'

'What does he do with himself all day, then?' Roland asked.

'He gets the odd job here and there – casual labour, I think. He doesn't talk about it much.'

I suddenly had the impression I'd said something that interested them very much. What on earth could it have been? The young man uncrossed his arms and lifted his chin, and Roland took the fountain-pen out again, uncapped it and held it poised.

'When was the last time he had a casual job?'

'Last week. That's why he couldn't visit Daniel in hospital. His son.'

'What kind of job was it?'

'I don't know,' I said.

'In Brussels?'

'Antwerp. That's all I know about it.'

There was a moment's silence. Then Roland said, 'About Daniel ... Mr Vanderauwera doesn't seem to have shown much interest in the child.'

Oh God, here we go.

'Luc isn't Daniel's real father,' I said. 'According to Marie-Paule, Daniel's father is Olivier Delfosse.'

'Madame Vanderauwera's ... friend?' Roland said.

I nodded.

22

'An unusual situation. Would you say Mr Vanderauwera held a grudge against his wife for that?'

I knew that Luc did.

'I think it would be only natural,' I said.

'Enough for him to consider murdering her?'

'She told him about it several years ago. Why wait till now to murder her?' I said.

The young man stood up, hands in pockets. 'Because she was threatening to sue him for a great deal of money, which he hasn't got. He uttered threats against her in the presence of witnesses in the hospital. And now you say he's held a grudge against her for years?'

'If my experience is anything to go by,' I said, 'you could fill Heysel Stadium with people who had grudges against Marie-Paule. Ask Luc where he was this afternoon.'

'We have,' Roland said gently. 'He says he was "driving around". He can't produce anyone to corroborate it. Incidentally, does he still have his Browning automatic?'

'What?' I asked.

Roland repeated, 'A Browning automatic is registered in his name. Does he still have it?'

'I don't know. Was that what she was shot with?'

Roland ignored my question. Instead, he said, 'You said he went out this morning in response to a phone call?'

'Yes,' I said patiently.

'And yet he denies anything of the sort. He says it was a call from a prospective buyer about something he wanted to sell. Needless to say, he didn't take the person's name or number. Well, one doesn't, does one?'

I remembered the urgency of Luc's tone on the phone that morning and the request not to call my apartment again. My confusion must have been evident. They glanced at one another. Roland capped the fountain-pen with a brisk movement and put it into his inside breast pocket.

23

'So why should he be lying?' he asked.

'What makes you think he is?' I protested.

'He told us he hasn't had any work since he left the police force. But you, on the other hand, say he's been doing casual jobs now and then. I prefer to believe you.'

My voice was a mere squeak. 'But why on earth should he lie about that?'

'Because he's been claiming unemployment benefit all this time,' Roland said cheerfully, 'which, as you probably know, isn't allowed. And if he lied about that, what else is he lying about?'

And I dropped him right in it, I thought grimly.

They kept me hanging about for another hour, then let me go. The first person I saw in the corridor outside was Luc. He looked pale and tense. He saw me, marched over and seized my arm.

'I've got to talk to you,' he said. 'Let's get outside.'

Behind us, Roland's voice said, 'Just a couple more things before you go, Mr Vanderauwera. Would you care to tell us again why you were in Antwerp last week?'

There was absolutely no hesitation in Luc's voice.

'How many more times?' he said irritably. 'I went on a blinder with some friends and spent most of the time drunk.'

'But that's not what you told Miss Haycastle,' Roland said gently.

'Yes, well, I didn't tell Matilda because I didn't want to worry her,' Luc said.

If that was true, I was Gazza's knee. Luckily for him, I was speechless. I don't know what my face looked like. But Roland hadn't done yet.

'Just one more question. Do you still have your Browning automatic?'

Luc's hand on my arm suddenly became very still. There was a silence which seemed to last for ever. Then he said, 'It's been stolen. I haven't had time to report it.'

Because I knew Luc well, I knew without a shadow of

a doubt that he was lying. I stared at him aghast.

'I see,' Roland said, looking at me. 'Don't leave the country, Mr Vanderauwera. We'll need to talk to you again.'

'Come on,' Luc muttered, pulling me down the corridor.

Outside in the street, he said, 'What did you tell them?'

'I told them what happened. Luc, what's going on? Where were you this afternoon?'

He didn't answer. He was frowning. 'You told them about the job in Antwerp?'

'Yes,' I answered miserably. 'I didn't know you were claiming the dole as well. I wish you'd told me.'

'You wouldn't have approved,' he said drily. 'Don't worry. That's the least of my troubles right now. Christ, what a mess.'

He rubbed both hands over his face and took a deep breath.

'But why can't you just tell them where you were today?' I said again.

'Just leave it, Matilda. Listen, your car's parked outside your place. The police were waiting for me there. Here are the keys. I'm going home. I'm dead beat. I'll call you, OK?'

OK. I watched him walk off down the street. I suddenly realized how tired I was. Getting home seemed to be a monumental task.

Behind me, Marius Charpentier said, 'At the risk of becoming a nuisance, may I offer you a lift? I'm taking Consuela home. Would you care to join the party or will you be independent and take a bus?'

We deposited Consuela at her sister's house, as the forensic team was still working at Marie-Paule's. Consuela was humbly grateful to Marius for the lift; I don't think she was used to such consideration.

'This is all a dastardly ploy to find out your address,'

25

Marius said, getting back into the car. I had to smile, little though I felt like it.

'You should try asking,' I said, and told him.

After driving for a moment or two in silence, he said suddenly, 'How's your alibi, by the way?'

'Solid, fortunately. I never thought I'd be grateful for one of my mother's phone calls. What about you?'

'Fifty witnesses. Hospitals aren't exactly private places. I suppose you realize who's first in line as a possible suspect?'

'Luc,' I said, heavily. 'That's all they seemed interested in.'

'Do you think he could have done it? He looks quite capable of it to me.'

'He could have,' I said. 'But I don't think he did. He went out for quite another reason and he's lying about it.'

'Tell me if I'm out of line, but am I right in thinking that your relationship is on the way out?'

'Are you a mind-reader?' I asked, rather ruefully.

'You don't have to be a mind-reader, just moderately observant. It's written all over you both.'

'Oh,' I said. 'Well, since you ask, yes, it is. But I still don't believe he killed his wife.'

'I wouldn't have blamed him if he had,' Marius observed, taking a corner with extreme care.

'I'm glad you said it and not me. But I don't understand why—' I broke off.

'Why he's lying?' Marius finished, matter-of-factly.

'Yes,' I said. 'But I'm going to find out.'

We came to a stop in front of my apartment block. Marius said, 'Would it be any help if I got hold of the autopsy report?'

'Can you?' I said, struggling with the seat-belt, which had got itself into a sort of granny knot.

'The police doctor's a colleague of mine,' he said. 'I'll plead professional interest. What's the point of having contacts if you don't use them?'

I succeeded in getting free of the belt and pushed the car door open with an effort.

'If you don't mind some professional advice,' Marius said, 'have a hot milky drink and go straight to bed. You look exhausted.'

'A double gin and tonic's what I need,' I said. 'Thanks for the lift. Thanks for everything.'

'That's a doctor's life for you. Always giving good advice and having it ignored. I'll be in touch.'

Chapter Four

There was no sign of life from any quarter for the next two days. I had a day and a half's work stuffing envelopes for a massive publicity mailing and came home on Tuesday night with aching shoulders and cut fingers. As I was feeding Hortense, the phone rang. Marius.

'I found your number,' he said unnecessarily. 'You're the only Haycastle in Brussels. I've got the report, so if you've nothing better to do tonight, why don't you come round?'

'OK. What time?'

'How about now? I'm making dinner, if you're interested.'

He lived in a turn-of-the-century terraced house in Watermael-Boitsfort, one of the leafy south-eastern suburbs. It was a narrow, pleasantly villagey street with neat little front gardens, a children's playground and a railway line not far away. Marius opened the door with a chopping knife in one hand. He had a plastic apron on, with a recipe for *tarte aux poires* on the front. It occurred to me that he was the most unselfconscious man I'd ever met. Luc wouldn't have worn an apron if his life depended on it.

'Come in. Help yourself to a glass of wine,' Marius said, waving the chopping knife vaguely at the dining-room table. 'I'm in the kitchen. Oh, did I mention that I'm a vegetarian?' He hadn't, but it didn't surprise me.

Sitting-room, dining-room and kitchen were in a line from the front to the back of the house. The whole of the back wall of the kitchen was a large picture window; there was just enough light left to see the garden, bordered on both sides by lilac bushes and running up to a clump of tall trees. Through the bare branches, I could see the tiled roofs of the houses on the next street – in the summer, the whole view must be one mass of green.

'What a wonderful view,' I said, walking through, a glass of wine in my hand. The kitchen table was covered with potato peelings. There was a small grey and white cat sitting on the window-sill outside.

'Yours?' I asked.

'Next-door's,' Marius said, going to open the back door. The cat strolled in, paused briefly to consider me, then disappeared upstairs with the air of one who knew the way.

'She sleeps here,' Marius said. 'I haven't the heart to throw her out these cold nights. The neighbours don't seem to bother about her much.'

We talked about cats and gardening while the dinner was cooking, then sat down and ate it. It was excellent. I'll never again say vegetarian food is boring. We had asparagus, a large, cheesey *gratin dauphinois* with crisp green salad, and a home-made fruit pie. I don't know where he'd found the time. We were interrupted twice by telephone calls, presumably from patients. While Marius was getting the coffee, I took a good look round. The house was mostly furnished in unvarnished pine, bamboo, wicker-work and natural fabrics. Green plants occupied all the spare space. There was a refreshing absence of knick-knackery. There was no sign of any feminine occupancy whatever. Bookshelves lined the dining-room walls, fiction and non-fiction, on an astounding range of subjects. Three whole shelves were taken up with comic strips.

'Are you a BD freak?' I called into the kitchen.

'How long have you lived in Belgium?' Marius asked. 'This is the home of Tintin, Lucky Luke and the Schtroumpfs. It's compulsory to like BDs.'

'Well, I've seen them in the bookshops,' I said, taking one down and opening it. It was science-fantasy, beautifully drawn, wildly surrealistic. This was a far cry from the *Beano*. Marius came back with the coffee pot to find me absorbed.

'Aha!' he said. 'I should warn you they're addictive.'

'Belgium never ceases to amaze me,' I said, closing the book and replacing it.

'Why? We've got some of the best surrealist painters in the world and BDs are just another form of art. There's a BD museum in Brussels – you should go. I should go, but I never seem to have the time. That's my medical section. Milk?'

Among the medical books I found three by one M. Charpentier.

'Are you famous?' I asked.

'I think I can say with all due modesty that I'm reasonably well known in certain circles,' he said.

I smiled. 'What's your speciality?'

'Traumatology,' he said. 'I practise privately for three days a week and spend three in the hospital.'

'What about weekends?'

'Weekends are a luxury unknown to doctors. That's the thing my wife found hardest to take.'

'Your wife?' I asked, leaving the books and coming back to the table.

'I'm divorced. Ten years ago. Quite amicably. I still see her sometimes. She's remarried and has a houseful of kids. Now, to business.'

He didn't want to talk about his wife. He reached to take a document from the shelf behind him, and frowned at it.

'I'll skip the technical stuff,' he said. 'Basically the subject was in good health, though her cholesterol levels

30

were rather high and she was carrying too much body-fat. Appendix and tonsils removed, probably as a child, blah blah blah. Death occurred between one-thirty and two o'clock from a gunshot wound as near the heart as makes no matter. One 9mm bullet recovered. Death was instantaneous. She must have fallen where she was standing. There are two circumstances which will no doubt excite the police: she had had sexual intercourse just prior to her death, and she had been sniffing coke. It was found on her skin and on the robe she was wearing. From the state of her nasal membranes, it was a habit of fairly long standing. There were no external signs of violence.'

'She must have had a *rendez-vous galant*,' I said slowly. 'Which explains why Consuela had the day off and Daniel was at his grandparents. But surely that exonerates Luc? It's much more likely to have been Olivier – he's the *amant en titre*, after all.'

'Wait a minute,' Marius cautioned. 'Firstly, it wasn't necessarily the man who slept with her who killed her. Secondly, are you sure it couldn't have been Luc? They're still married, after all, and people do the most bizarre things. In any case, we'll soon know, because the police will no doubt haul both gentlemen in for tests.'

I sat staring grimly at my coffee cup, aware that I was no longer sure of anything about Luc, and hating myself for it.

'I don't want to be intrusive,' Marius said, 'but what are you planning to do?'

'Investigate Marie-Paule. She's the key to it all,' I said slowly. 'She's the one who's been responsible for the whole mess. She pulled all those people's lives out of their orbits: Luc, Olivier, Olivier's family, even mine.'

'And Daniel's,' Marius reminded me. 'The child has two completely different personae. A meek, obedient, polite little boy while his mother's around, and the normal, extremely bright, self-sufficient child that you saw. Startlingly self-sufficient for ten. He switches between them at will. A remarkable case of protective camouflage.'

'And who knows how many other people's lives she's messed about with?' I went on. 'And how come she's got a beautiful house with a live-in maid and expensive clothes when eight months ago she and Luc and Daniel were living off a policeman's salary?'

'Wealthy parents?'

'Maybe. And maybe it's Olivier. Although he's got a wife and kids to support too, if I'm not mistaken. So where's the money coming from? I definitely feel an attack of nosey-parkerism is imminent. I'm going to talk to a few people.'

'Well, if there's anything I can do to help, let me know,' Marius said. 'And mind you keep me informed. You're not the only nosey-parker around.'

I approached Marie-Paule's house with some trepidation the next day in case representatives of the law were still hanging about, but the Avenue Molière looked peaceful and prosperous, as it usually does. Consuela opened the door with a worried and rather frightened expression, which cleared up instantly when she saw me. I'd prepared a little spiel to get myself into the house, but it wasn't necessary. She whisked me inside with smiles and inviting gestures and immediately began thanking me all over again for the lift home from the police station. I blessed Marius's kind heart for doing me a good turn.

Consuela spoke reasonably good French, though with a heavy accent. The effusive thanks led to the offer of a cup of coffee, and five minutes later we were sitting at the kitchen table. She was overwhelmingly grateful to have someone to talk to. Not surprising, if she'd been sitting alone in that empty house with nothing to do.

She looked like a countrywoman: decent, hardworking, uncomplicated. She was dressed in a black skirt and sweater, with a gold cross round her neck on a chain. Her hand kept returning again and again to the cross, all through our conversation. Her worried brown eyes kept darting to my face and away again. She told me how frightened she'd been of the police. They'd kept on asking her questions about Marie-Paule and she'd hardly known what to say.

'They asked me questions too,' I said, reassuringly. 'Mr Vanderauwera is my friend and they think he must have had something to do with it. But I'm sure he didn't. That's why I want to talk to you. I need your help.'

The brown eyes settled on me at last. 'How can I help?' she asked. She had a low, rather harsh voice.

'There are things I need to know about Madame Vanderauwera. For example, did she own this house? How long have you been working for her?'

'I've been here for six months,' she said, holding up six fingers for confirmation. 'Ever since Madame bought the house. I told the police that.'

'I didn't know Madame Vanderauwera very well. Was she a good employer?'

The frightened expression came back to the plain face. She stared at me, her fingers clenched hard on the cross at her throat. On an impulse, I said, 'Listen, Consuela. I'm not from the police. I'm not particularly fond of them myself. I just want to get at the truth. I promise I won't repeat anything you say to anybody. But you're the person who must have known the most about her.'

There was a long silence. Finally, her eyes cast down, she said slowly, 'She wasn't a – good – woman. Her family didn't know. If they ever hear I told you this, they'll have me sent back to Spain.'

'They won't hear of it,' I said.

'Madame's father,' she said, staring at me, 'he was a policeman. He's a rich man and I'm poor. I need this job – my family in Spain is large. My brothers must be educated.'

'I swear I won't tell anyone,' I said.

'On the cross?' she asked suddenly, unexpectedly.

'I'm not a Catholic,' I said. 'But I'll swear on the cross, if you want.'

That seemed to convince her. She stared at me for a moment longer, then said suddenly, 'There were men. Different men. Sometimes they would come here, sometimes she would go out. She was a bad woman.'

'They'd come here?' I asked incredulously. 'But what about Olivier – Monsieur Delfosse?'

She shrugged. 'He's married. He has a wife and three little girls, God forgive him. He came here only on certain days, at certain times. She insisted on that. At other times, there were the others. Sometimes even with the child in the house. What a mother! Poor little boy.'

'Did he know what was going on?'

'She tried to hide it from him, but I think Daniel sees too much.'

'And what about that Sunday? Did she have a visitor then?'

'I think so. On Sunday, she was always alone in the house. For a while now there has been a young man. Not a very nice young man. He comes to her on Sunday. On God's own day, imagine.'

'What does he look like?' I asked.

'Young. Like a student. The long hair, the jeans, the running-shoes. He looks impudent – bad.'

'Hair colour?'

She tried to think. 'Brown. Like yours.'

'Eyes?'

She didn't know. She'd only seen him a couple of times.

'Do you know his name?'

She shook her head.

'Can you tell me anything else about him?'

There was another long pause. Then she said: 'He brought her the drugs she used. He brought her all kinds

34

of pills and powders – they used them together.'

'Hard drugs?' I asked.

She shook her head. 'Madame took many pills but she didn't inject herself,' she said. 'There were no marks on her. I would have seen them. I don't know about him. Many of the young people do it here in Belgium. It's a terrible thing.'

'What kind of pills?' I asked.

'Many pills.' Consuela said, shrugging. 'The police took them all away.'

'Did Madame Vanderauwera know you knew all this?'

'Oh yes,' Consuela said, with a sad little smile. 'She told me that if I ever said anything, she'd accuse me of stealing and have me arrested. Then I'd go to prison.'

I looked at her and said gently, 'I understand that you're frightened, but you know, you really should go to the police about all this. I think it might be very important.'

She looked at me for a long moment with those dense brown eyes. 'I went to confession,' she said. 'Not to my own church. I went to a place where no one knew me. The priest said the same, that I should go to the police. I know you're right. But I'm afraid.'

'They can't send you back to Spain. You're an EC citizen, you can look for another job here. A job where you're treated properly. I know people who can help you.'

'You're very kind,' she said, but I might have saved myself the bother. She wasn't convinced. To people like Consuela, the rich and influential always win out over the poor and unconnected, and all the European Community Directives in the world don't make tuppence worth of difference.

She looked round at the shining tiled walls and added, 'It's very sad here now. I don't want to stay. Everything has changed. And Daniel's not here any more.'

'He's staying with his grandparents?' I asked.

She nodded sadly. 'I miss him very much,' she said.

'There's just one more thing,' I said. 'May I take a look round the house before I go? You don't mind?'

'No. But there's nothing to see now.'

But there was. The top floor consisted of Consuela's own room, small but comfortable, Daniel's bedroom and playroom, and a bathroom which they shared. Daniel's rooms were decorated and furnished in a rather babyish style for a ten-year-old boy and had almost no character. A few battered soft toys sat leaning together on a shelf, oddly forlorn. Consuela automatically straightened them up, but they promptly leaned tiredly together again; after a while, the stuffing in the legs goes.

'There would have been trouble, later,' she said. 'She didn't want him to grow up, but how do you stop a child from becoming a man?'

I'd expected luxury in Marie-Paule's own rooms, and I wasn't wrong. In fact, the luxury was almost ludicrous, like a cliché filmset for a bad movie about Hollywood: fur carpet, king-size bed, silk sheets, mirrors, the lot. The bathroom was about the size of my living-room at home, with sunken bath, jacuzzi and various other gadgets, the purpose of which I hardly dared guess at. Her clothes had a room all to themselves. Imelda Marcos would have been green with envy. Marie-Paule must have spent a fortune just dressing herself. Looking through the silk dresses and fur coats, I wondered again where the money was coming from. Olivier? He must be absolutely rolling in it. I wondered cynically whether he set these expenses off against his income tax. Maybe there was a special rate for mistresses.

'The jewels are in the bank,' Consuela said softly behind me. Of course, there would be jewels.

Awed by the ostentation, I followed Consuela downstairs. The dining-room, expensively and formally furnished, looked as if it hadn't been used much. There was a small office, a hall, and the living-room where we had found the body. I must say I felt a bit odd about going in there. I half expected to see bloodstains on the carpet, but of course, there was nothing. In fact, the carpet was brand-new. It was a pleasant room, well lit by a large bow window overlooking the garden. A writing desk and chair stood in the window. The furniture was expensive, of course; the table lamps alone would probably have bought all the furniture in my flat. There was a marble fireplace which had never seen a real fire, and, hanging over it, a poster-sized portrait of Marie-Paule herself.

The portrait caught my attention immediately, because it struck a completely discordant note in all that heavy luxury. I went up close and stood on tip-toe to see. It was clearly an original and must have been done ten or twelve years previously, before Marie-Paule's excesses had started to show on her face. She was young, laughing, happy, slouching in an armchair, one knee up over the arm of the chair. Her hair was long and luxurious, contrasting with the dull black of the leather jacket she had on. The whole picture had an air of immediacy, an excitement, that was quite its own. The colours were clear and spring-like, the execution finely detailed. It was an unusual piece of work. I craned my neck to see if it was signed, but the only obvious thing was a squiggle in the bottom left-hand corner, nearly under the frame. It looked like an ornate 'J', but I couldn't be sure.

'Monsieur Delfosse didn't like that painting,' Consuela said, making me jump. I'd forgotten she was there. 'He wanted Madame to dispose of it.'

'It's lovely,' I said. 'She looks so different.'

I went to look out of the window. The garden was beautifully landscaped; clusters of snowdrops danced in the wind and the tulips were pushing up already. A leather-bound diary lay open on the desk, at today's date, though Marie-Paule would never use it again. I idly flipped back through the pages. There was nothing except a couple of appointments during the week before she died: Coiffeur Rosalie on Monday afternoon, Doctor Goldstein on Wednesday morning. I noted the names and dates, then closed the book gently and turned.

'I think I'd better be going. Thank you for being so helpful. If there's anything I can ever do for you, please call me.'

Consuela looked rather doubtful at this, but I left my address and phone number anyway and went home. The phone was ringing as I got in. It was my temp agency, rather peeved at the fact that I hadn't been in all day. I'd missed a good contract. All they could offer for the rest of the week was a couple of days typing labels. I accepted. What else could I do?

'You can forget the gourmet meals for a while, H,' I said to Hortense. 'It'll be Kit-e-Kat for both of us if this goes on much longer.'

Luc called that evening. I hadn't seen or heard from him since the night of the murder. I wanted to sort things out between us, but it was a difficult subject to get round to.

'The funeral's on Saturday,' he said. 'Do you want to go?'

He sounded as if he'd rather I didn't.

'Do you want me to?' I asked. Funerals aren't exactly my idea of a fun way to spend an afternoon. There was a long pause.

'Well, I think I'd find it easier if you didn't,' he said finally. 'If you don't mind.'

'No, I don't mind. Listen, Luc, I have to see you. We've got to talk.'

'Matilda, things are just too difficult at the moment. Can it wait till after the funeral? I've got a million things to sort out, what with lawyers crawling all over me and the police still on my back. I've even had to go down to the bloody hospital and give samples.'

'What samples?' I said without thinking.

'Use your head,' he replied derisively. 'They want to know who slept with her before she died.'

38

'Oh,' I said.

'I promise I'll be in touch over the weekend. OK?'

It would have to be OK, wouldn't it? I was conscious of irritation. Having made my mind up to do the thing, it was annoying to be forced to put it off. I thought with some grimness that as far as Luc was concerned, our personal dilemma must rank way below his other headaches at the moment.

Chapter Five

Typing labels is one of my least favourite jobs in the universe. All the same, I wasn't exactly pleased to be interrupted on Thursday morning by a call from the police. The telephone girl's hushed tones as she announced the call told me exactly what she thought of it all; I could see her staring at me through the glass partition between the offices. It was Inspector Lebrun, the rude young man who'd been present at my interview. Commissaire Roland wished to see me that afternoon.

'I'm working,' I protested. 'I can't get down there till after six.'

'Make an effort,' he said.

'Listen, I'm perfectly prepared to cooperate with you, but I have to earn my living. If I come down now, I'll lose money. Is Commissaire Roland willing to compensate me? Perhaps you'd be good enough to ask him?'

There was a silence at the other end. Then: 'Do you want us to send a car down to get you?' he said nastily.

I really don't like being pushed around, especially by arrogant young men.

'That'll just about give me time to ring my lawyer,' I told him.

There was a confused noise at the other end, followed by a clunk, and then another voice, which I recognized: Commissaire Roland's.

'My young man seems to be having a little communication problem,' he said cheerfully. 'When can you come down?'

I explained.

'When's your lunch-hour?' Roland said. 'I'll come to you. Where are you working?'

I suggested we meet at twelve-thirty in a café near the office.

'Fine,' he said, 'I'll see you then. Have a nice day.'

What was this all about?

At the reception desk, the telephone girl and another secretary were already in a huddle. By the end of the morning, the whole office would be in on it. I got up and went out to the ladies' room. As I passed reception, I said, 'I'm part of an international drug-smuggling ring,' and had the satisfaction of seeing two jaws drop simultaneously.

Roland was already in the café when I got there. It was a typical lunch-time place: *plats du jour* being served at the speed of light to a crowd of office-workers. Roland was reading *Le Soir*. He folded the paper up as I came in, and smiled. He looked friendly enough.

We exchanged greetings and ordered lunch. Then Roland said, 'Consuela Garcia came to see us today. I gather we have you to thank for that.'

'I think the Catholic church gets some credit,' I said.

He smiled. 'Possibly. What made you go and talk to her?'

'Curiosity,' I said. 'I wanted to find out more about Marie-Paule. I know almost nothing about her, except what Luc's told me. Did Consuela tell you there was another man there on Sunday?'

'Yes. And I'm inclined to believe her. Madame Vanderauwera had a lover there that day and the forensic tests have shown it was neither Vanderauwera nor Delfosse.'

I felt hot with relief. Marius Charpentier's suggestion that it might have been Luc who'd slept with Marie-

Paule that day had unnerved me more than I cared to admit.

Roland went on: 'However, that doesn't mean one of them didn't kill her. Neither of them has been able to come up with a satisfactory alibi. Monsieur Delfosse says he was walking his dog in the forest. Since the dog can't talk, we've been unable to verify it. And as for Vanderauwera, we're no wiser. What about you?'

'He won't talk about it,' I said. 'I haven't seen him since we left the police station, and he's only called me once.'

Food appeared. We started to eat. I looked at the bland face across the table and wondered what I was being softened up for.

'Did you know that your friend Mr Vanderauwera has already killed two men?' Roland asked, quite casually.

I didn't know. I put my knife and fork down, feeling a little queasy.

'Oh, in the line of duty, of course,' the Commissaire went on airily. 'He was working on a drugs case a few years back and it turned nasty. But it proves he's quite capable of killing. According to her parents, he'd threatened her several times.'

'They're not exactly unbiased witnesses, though, are they?' I said, finding my voice. 'Divorces bring out the worst in people, anyway – one says things one doesn't mean.'

'Ah, yes. They weren't divorced yet, were they? You realize that legally he's entitled to a share of her estate?'

'How much did she have?' I asked.

He smiled, but didn't answer.

'He can't produce his gun, so we're unable to make tests to see if the bullet came from it or not. That's a great pity. And then, there's the lack of alibi. You'd be doing your friend a great service if you could persuade him to tell us where he was on Sunday.'

'Luc hasn't told me anything,' I said. 'Anyway, I

42

thought you said Olivier Delfosse hadn't got an alibi either? Why isn't he on your list of suspects?'

'I didn't say he wasn't. But where's his motive?'

'He must have been spending a fortune on Marie-Paule – the house, the clothes and so on. Maybe the money was running out?'

Roland shook his head gently.

'I'm afraid not. Monsieur Delfosse is unequivocally well off. There's money in the family. He admits quite freely that he had every intention of marrying Madame Vanderauwera once her divorce was through. He and his wife are already legally separated.'

'And how did his wife feel about that? If anyone had a reason to hate Marie-Paule, she did. Have you asked her where she was on Sunday?'

'Naturally. She was at the coast with her children. Her alibi's as solid as yours. Incidentally, did you know that Delfosse has decided to claim paternity of the Vanderauwera child?'

I looked up, startled. 'He can't, surely, after ten years? Isn't there a legal time-limit?'

Roland shrugged. 'The law isn't all that clear. Delfosse says he's got papers signed by Marie-Paule which prove Daniel is his son and he's asked for genetic tests to be made. With a clever lawyer, he might succeed. The grandparents are fighting it.'

'Oh, for Heaven's sake!' I exclaimed. 'Why can't he leave the poor child alone? It seems to me that the last person anybody's thinking about is Daniel. As if it isn't enough that his mother's just been murdered!'

'You're fond of him?' he asked, looking at me curiously.

'I don't think he's been getting a very fair deal,' I said.

My lunch was getting cold. Roland had finished his already. Now he sat back and studied me with all the appearance of amiability.

'I think you could help us if you tried,' he said. 'We

really need that information on Vanderauwera.'

'I told you. Luc hasn't said a word to me,' I said finally. 'And frankly, the way things are between us now, I hardly expect he will. But if I can find out anything, I'll let you know.'

'That's all we can ask,' he said cheerfully. 'And keep these latest revelations under your hat. We promised Madame Garcia confidentiality.'

Back in the office, I had another surprise. Olivier Delfosse was sitting in the reception area, a briefcase on his knees, staring into space. He was wearing his camel-hair overcoat and smelled of money. As I walked through the door, he leapt to his feet and said eagerly, 'Mademoiselle Haycastle? May I have a word?'

'Sure,' I said, stopping. What in the world did he want?

Seen up close, it was a rather open, uncomplicated face, with brown dog's eyes and that eternal five o'clock shadow. He didn't look like a murderer. But then, what does a murderer look like?

'How did you find me?' I asked.

'The police,' he said. 'I hope you don't mind. I just felt I had to come and thank you on Daniel's behalf. You know, for coming to the hospital, bringing the book and so on. It was very kind of you.'

'That's OK,' I said, a little surprised. 'How is Daniel?'

'He's fine. It was a shock, of course, but children are very resilient.'

He hesitated, shot me a look, then said, 'I expect you think I'm wrong trying to get Daniel back?'

I did, but I could hardly say so. Instead I said, 'It's none of my business.'

'Everybody else thinks so,' he said gloomily. There was a rather child-like quality about this big man. He looked at me with those pleading dark-brown eyes.

'He's my son,' he said. 'My son. I love him. I want him. You see, my other children are all daughters, and my wife couldn't have any more.'

I stared in amazement. Did he really think that was an

excuse to toss them all out on the street? Then with a slight shock, I saw that there were tears in his eyes. An emotional man. I remembered the gift he had given Daniel so eagerly in the hospital, and equally remembered Daniel's lukewarm response. That must have hurt him. But as I'd said, it wasn't any of my business.

'I'm sure it'll all work out for the best,' I said. 'The best for Daniel, that is. That's the important thing.'

'Yes, you're right,' he said. 'That's what she would have liked. That's all I can do for her now.'

His eyes filled with tears again, and he wiped them away with the flat of his hand, just like a child.

'I'm sorry,' he said. 'I just can't get used to it.' He stopped and looked down, gulped, then seemed to take his courage in both hands. 'You – you saw her, didn't you? I mean, you found her – that day? Did she – did she look as if she'd suffered any pain?'

So that was what was really on his mind. Poor mutt. He was the only one who'd really loved her. I couldn't stop myself putting a sympathetic hand on his arm.

'No,' I said firmly. 'Death was instantaneous; she can't have suffered at all.'

It seemed to satisfy him. He swallowed, nodded a couple of times, pressed my hand and then seized his briefcase and made off through the door.

The labels occupied me till the end of the week. I tried and failed to get hold of Marius Charpentier. I had an idea he might be just the person to advise me about tracking down drug dealers, but I had to be content with leaving messages all over town.

On Saturday morning the phone rang.

'Ah!' I thought.

A small voice said, 'Mathilde?'

Daniel?

Amazed, I said, 'Yes, it's me. Is that Daniel? How are you?'

'Fine. Mathilde, can I talk to you?'

'Of course. What's the matter?'

'I can't talk now,' he said. 'Can you meet me in the park? We're going there after lunch today.'

'Which park?'

'The Abbaye de la Cambre. Do you know it?'

'Yes. What time?'

There was a pause. 'After lunch,' Daniel said again.

'What time do you usually have lunch?'

'Twelve o'clock.'

'All right. I'll be there.'

'Thank you. I have to go.' The phone clattered down.

What's this, Matilda? Assignations in parks with ten-year-olds? What are things coming to?

I went out at one o'clock. The Abbaye de la Cambre is a small green lung near the top of the Avenue Louise. A deep hollow in the land shelters the remains of an old abbey and a pretty landscaped garden. Tall buildings tower cliff-like all round and the traffic roars round the outside, but down in the hollow, it's surprisingly peaceful. I found Daniel kicking a ball in an alley of pollarded trees. He ran to me and took my hand.

'Maria's over there,' he said, indicating a park bench on which two bundled-up figures were chatting animatedly. 'She meets her sister here while I play. I'll go and tell her who you are.'

Two elderly ladies of Mediterranean extraction ceased their rapid chatter and listened, staring at me with beady interested eyes, while Daniel explained I was a friend and we were going to play for a while. I smiled and nodded like one of those wind-up toys, and the ladies smiled and nodded too.

'That was easy,' Daniel said, leading me away. 'Maria's not very clever.'

'How did you get my number?' I asked.

'The phone book,' Daniel said, looking at me in surprise. 'Everybody's out today.'

I remembered that his mother was being buried that

46

day. Daniel looked surprisingly untouched by it all. He led me to another bench and we sat down.

'I wanted to talk to you about Olivier,' he said. 'He says he's my father.'

'Yes, I heard,' I said. A weak sun was shining. In that sheltered spot, it was nice and warm. Pigeons were cooing hopefully in the bare trees around.

'I don't want Olivier to be my father,' he said. 'Mamie and Papie don't want it either. I want to stay with them now. Mamie says I can have a dog.'

'Don't you like Olivier?' I asked gently.

'He's all right,' Daniel said. 'But I don't want to go and live with him. And how can he be my father? He doesn't even look like me.'

'They won't send you to live with him unless they're absolutely certain that he is your father and that living with him is the best thing for you,' I said. 'I'm sure they'll ask you what you prefer. And anyway, it'll all take a long, long time.'

'But how will they know?' Daniel asked, looking at me.

Studying the straight-featured little face with its clear grey eyes and silver hair, I reflected that Daniel was right; it was a totally different physical type from Olivier's heavy swarthiness. But children change, of course.

'There are medical tests they can do,' I said. 'People who are related have similar cell structure – they're made out of the same material.'

'Oh.' Daniel thought about this for a minute. Then he said, 'I'd rather have Luc as a father. Is he going to do the tests too?'

'I don't know. Would you like him to?'

Daniel nodded. 'Maman said he wasn't my father, but maybe she was wrong,' he said hopefully. 'I thought maybe you could ask him.'

So that was it.

'I'll try, but he's very busy at the moment,' I said gently.

47

'He's always busy,' Daniel said.

We were interrupted by the arrival of a dachshund, which came dashing up, investigated all the legs of the bench, and started sniffing at Daniel's shoes. His face lit up; he got down on the ground with it and reached out confidently to pat it. The dachshund leapt up enthusiastically to lick his face, then rushed off in response to a piercing whistle from the other side of the park.

'I'm going to have one of those,' he said, getting up and solemnly dusting down the knees of his trousers. It didn't help much. 'I really like them. I've always wanted a dog of my own. Mamie says we can go and buy it next week.'

'You like living with your grandparents?' I asked.

He nodded enthusiastically.

'Mamie lets me have posters on the walls of my room,' he said. 'I've got the Ninja Mutant Turtles and Madonna. I think she's really pretty.'

'Yes,' I said, thanking Heaven that innocence still existed.

'And I'm going skiing with the school soon,' he went on. Then he stopped and looked at me seriously for a moment.

'I do miss Maman, you know,' he said, 'but not as much as I thought I would.'

I thought about that rather savagely as I drove home.

Chapter Six

Saturday afternoon went by with no word from Luc. Early on Sunday afternoon the doorbell rang. At last! I pressed the buzzer to open the downstairs door, left my front door ajar and went to make coffee, rapidly trying to marshal my thoughts. I'd been rehearsing this conversation to myself all weekend. There was no need for things to get nasty if we both behaved sensibly.

A diffident voice said, 'May I come in?'

It was Marius Charpentier. As I gaped in surprise, Hortense shot out of the front door and disappeared down the stairs, tail raised in triumph.

'Your cat just left,' Marius said.

'Leave the door open and she'll be back. She's playing at explorers. Come in. I didn't expect to see you. I thought it was someone else.'

'Are you expecting somebody? I can come back later.' He started to retreat towards the open door.

'No, not really. I'm making coffee. Would you like some?'

'I'd love some. I got all your messages. I'm sorry I didn't get back to you sooner. It's a busy time of year for me – lots of nice profitable skiing accidents.'

Hortense reappeared, looking smug, and made a bee-line for Marius. She likes men. I introduced them and they had a conversation while I was getting the coffee.

'Wonderful,' Marius said, sniffing appreciatively at his cup. 'What did you want to see me about?'

His directness was a relief. I ended up telling him everything that had happened. He listened without comment to the end. Then he said, 'You want to try and trace this young man with the habit? Frankly, without a name or a better description, it's virtually impossible. I suppose all the police have to go on is the forensic evidence? Well, they can hardly go round testing the body fluids of every young male drug addict in the country.'

'But if I could get a better description? I could talk to Consuela again.'

'Then there might be a chance. I have colleagues working in the drugs area – running shelters and so on. We might make enquiries there.'

'Maybe somebody else saw him, if he came to the house regularly. The neighbours, for instance?'

'Neighbours never see or hear a thing,' Marius said. 'Nobody even seems to have heard the shot that killed Marie-Paule. In fact, they all probably did, but put it down to a car back-firing or some such thing.'

'How do you know?' I asked, staring.

'The police have spoken to me again. They were enquiring about your relationship with Mr Vanderauwera. I pleaded total ignorance, which wasn't difficult.'

'They want Luc to tell them where he was on Sunday,' I said.

'And he won't?'

I shook my head.

'He should,' Marius said.

'I think maybe—' I said before I could stop myself. Marius finished the sentence for me.

' . . . he was doing something he doesn't want you to know about?'

'No. Something he doesn't want the police to know about.'

Marius said nothing but the expression on his face as he looked at me was one of speechless concern. To change the subject, I told him about Daniel and Olivier. He groaned.

'The sheer selfishness of it all. He must have his son, therefore never mind about the wife and the three little girls, Daniel or Daniel's grandparents. It's pathetic.'

'He seems to love Daniel very much,' I said musingly.

'Then he should think of what's best for him.' Marius stopped and sighed. 'I suppose it's easy for me to talk, with no kids of my own. Doctors are always telling other people what's best for them, but what do we really know in the end?'

'What's this?' I asked with a smile. 'Self-doubt?'

'It's like malaria; I get an attack every now and then. I can't help feeling I'm wasting my time dealing with skiing injuries and rich kids who break their necks falling out of hang-gliders.'

'So go and do something else,' I said. 'Go off to Somalia or Bosnia or somewhere. They could really use your skills there.'

He looked at me with an arrested air, but before he could answer, the doorbell rang again. Twice.

Luc.

Wouldn't you just know it?

I could hardly pretend not to be there. Luc came in with a preoccupied expression on his face, which changed instantly to one of hostility when he saw Marius. Marius stood up. If he'd had a beard, it would have bristled. They stared at one another belligerently, exactly like two tom-cats meeting in a garden. I sighed.

'You know Doctor Charpentier, I believe?' I asked.

'Yes, we've met.' Luc took off his jacket and threw it casually over the back of the sofa, as if he owned the place. 'Do you have any advice for me today, doctor?'

I felt unreasonably irritated, by the action as well as the words.

'Plenty,' Marius said. 'But I don't suppose for one minute you'd take it, so I'll spare myself the bother. I'll be going, Matilda. I've got a football match to referee. Let me know if you come up with anything new, and I'll do the same. Thanks for the coffee and good afternoon.'

The door closed behind him and Luc and I stared at one another in silence.

'Bossy individual,' Luc said. 'What's he sniffing around for?'

Calm down, I told myself. There's no point getting tetchy. 'He's not sniffing around. I needed his advice about something. The police have been on to me again.'

Luc made a snorting noise and sat down. He looked tired.

'What did they want? Your alibi's good, isn't it?'

'They want me to persuade you to tell them where you were. I said I didn't think there was much chance.'

He looked at me very intently, but said nothing. I folded my arms and stared back.

'Did you know Olivier's started proceedings to get custody of Daniel?' I asked.

'Yes. It was today's good news.'

'Are you going to do anything about it?'

'What do you suggest? I'm not the child's father. Let them get on with it.'

'Daniel told me today he doesn't want to live with Olivier. He'd prefer to have you as a father.'

'Yes, well it's a bit late for that,' Luc said bitterly.

'Isn't there even an off-chance that you might be?'

He gave me another of those searching looks. 'Matilda, what's all this about?' he asked.

I took a deep breath. 'Daniel wants you to take the tests as well. Just in case.'

'Oh, for God's sake,' Luc said tiredly. 'As if I didn't have enough on my plate. I've already been messed about by the police doctors – I'm certainly not about to put myself through any more procedures.'

'In case they find out you really are his father and you have to shoulder your responsibilities?' I said quietly.

There was a silence, then he said, 'Be careful, Matilda.'
I'd never seen his eyes so cold.

'Or what? Don't you even care enough for Daniel to do this for him?'

'Do you want to know how I really feel? I couldn't care less if I never see him again. I'm sick to death of Marie-Paule and everything to do with her.'

He got up in a violent movement and ranged over to the window to stare out.

'Where were you on Sunday?' I asked, and he whirled, his face furious.

'Goddamit, Matilda, don't you play the policeman with me. It's none of your bloody business.'

'I thought you trusted me.'

'I don't have to put up with this,' he said curtly. As he seized his jacket and made for the door, I said, 'If you go out of that door now, you needn't bother to come back.'

He stopped in the doorway and looked at me coldly. 'That suits me fine,' he said.

The door slammed.

And that was that. So much for behaving sensibly. After a while, I cheered up. At least it was settled.

I felt rather less cheerful that evening when I was tidying up for the start of the new week. There were bits and pieces of Luc's all over the flat. A sweater and a pair of socks in the bedroom. A packet of batteries which he'd bought and then left in the kitchen. A tin of shoe-polish. And his emergency overnight kit which he kept in my bathroom cabinet: electric razor and various odds and ends. I made a heap in the middle of the sitting-room floor and went to fetch a plastic bag to put everything in. The razor fell out of its half-unzipped case as I picked it up, together with the guarantee booklet and what looked like a folded-up bank-note. It *was* a folded-up bank-note. I sat down slowly on the carpet, staring at the unfamiliar printing. Zlotys! 50,000 of them. I picked up the guarantee booklet; with it was a cheap business card belonging

53

to a garage in Antwerp, with, on the reverse side, a pencilled address in Warsaw.

Warsaw?

So that was where he'd been. No wonder he'd had his passport with him.

But what the hell was Luc doing in Warsaw at this time of the year? Or at any time of the year? Well, at least I had a lead now.

Chapter Seven

Maddeningly, I couldn't do a damn thing about it the following week, because the agency came up with a job and I had to take it. The weather started, at last, to get marginally warmer. Hortense was moulting and had a cold. No news filtered through about the murder. On Friday night the telephone rang. It was Daniel, sounding buoyant.

'Mathilde, can you come to tea tomorrow?'

'Yes, I can. Where?'

'Here,' he said blithely. 'Chez Mamie.'

I hesitated. 'Are you sure your grandmother won't mind me coming, Daniel?'

I heard a confusion of voices at the other end, then a woman's voice, pleasant, rather hesitant.

'Mademoiselle Haycastle? I'm Agnès Gheyssens, Daniel's grandmother. Daniel would be very pleased if you could come tomorrow. Say three o'clock?'

'I'd love to,' I said. 'Thank you very much.'

'Until tomorrow, then,' she said. She gave me the address and rang off, leaving me somewhat perplexed. I didn't know much about Madame Gheyssens. Luc had hardly mentioned her. It was unusual, to say the least, that she would contemplate inviting to her house the rival of her recently murdered daughter. What was I letting myself in for this time?

I soon found out. The maid who answered the door (I was moving in high society these days) led me into a pleasant flower-filled living-room where I was greeted not by Daniel, but by a small elegant woman with delicate features and dark hair with just a touch of grey. She held out a slender hand and said, 'Daniel's waiting next door, but I wanted to meet you first. I wanted to thank you for persuading Luc to take those tests. He should have done it years ago.'

'He took the tests, then?' I exclaimed, startled. 'I didn't know – I didn't think he would. What was the result? Is Daniel his child?'

'No,' Agnès Gheyssens said, simply. She looked up at me hesitantly. 'You aren't at all what I expected,' she said. 'Daniel told me how kind you were. You seem to have been the only one in all this who cared what happened to him.'

'Apart from you,' I said.

'He's all I have left now,' she said simply. 'My daughter was always close to her father – they were very alike, you see. It's strange how you can become a complete stranger to your own flesh and blood, in your own house.'

There was a wealth of unhappiness in her voice, but I didn't know her well enough to be able to offer sympathy. Uncomfortably, I said, 'What happens to Daniel now? Will Olivier go on with his case?'

She looked up at me with her dark eyes. 'Of course, you don't know,' she said. 'The tests showed that Luc isn't Daniel's father. But neither is Olivier.'

I was still in a daze when the maid showed me into a sunny room at the back of the house, where Daniel was waiting. Just inside the door, I was set upon by a small brown creature the size of a bedroom slipper, which leapt, growling ferociously, onto my foot and began to worry my shoelaces. I bent to pick it up and the growls changed to ecstatic whines, while a flannel-like tongue licked the make-up off my nose.

'Hello, Mathilde,' said Daniel. 'This is Daisy. Daisy, this is Mathilde.'

It was a dachshund puppy, long-haired and perfectly adorable. I put her down, then sat on the sofa and wiped my face with my hanky, while the puppy rushed madly across to Daniel, bouncing like a little rubber ball.

'Isn't she beautiful?' Daniel said enthusiastically. His whole face was radiant with pleasure. 'She's got a much longer name because she's a very well-bred dog, but we just call her Daisy. She's excited because she hasn't met you before. I've got a basket for her, and a collar and lead, and some toys. I didn't know dogs could have toys.'

The maid, smiling, brought in a trolley full of the most gorgeous-looking pastries, and poured tea, while Daniel told me all about his projected skiing trip to Switzerland. He'd never been allowed to go away with the school before, and he couldn't wait. But the enthusiasm was carefully restrained. He had beautiful manners for a child of his age; almost too beautiful. His self-control had been learned too early and too well.

It wasn't till almost the end of tea that he mentioned the thing that had been foremost in my thoughts all afternoon. Daisy had fallen asleep, worn out with all the rushing about, and he was lying on his stomach stroking her soft ears. He looked up without warning and said, 'Olivier isn't my father after all.'

'So I hear,' I said. 'That must be a relief for you.'

'Yes, it is. Luc isn't my father either.'

'No. But you half knew that.'

'Yes. But it's a pity,' he said gravely.

There was a short silence, then he said, 'Mathilde?'

'Yes?'

'Will you find my father for me?'

My surprise must have shown on my face, because he hastily added, 'Luc says you're good at finding out things and there isn't anybody else I can ask. Please say yes, Mathilde.'

'Daniel, come here,' I said. He got up slowly and came and sat on the sofa with me.

57

'Now listen,' I said. 'First of all, it may not be possible to find out who he was after all this time. Secondly, even if we do find him, we have to be very careful – he may be surprised to find out about you, or he may have a wife and family. Or,' I added gently, 'he might even be dead.'

'Yes, I know,' Daniel said. 'It's just that I want to know who he is. And maybe he'd like to know about me. Will you, Mathilde, please?'

I took a deep breath. 'Well, I'll try,' I said.

Daniel clapped his hands and gave a little bounce. 'Oh, good,' he said. 'Thank you, Mathilde. Can you start straight away?'

'Can I have another cup of tea first?' I asked.

Chapter Eight

I sat down on Sunday morning with a map of Belgium and worked out a plan of campaign. I had no work scheduled this week, so I'd take advantage of my freedom. The Flanders offensive was about to begin.

My starting-place was Lier, Luc's home town. That was where he'd met and become involved with Marie-Paule, and since his family all still lived there, hopefully somebody might remember something. Maggie, his mother, was the obvious place to start. I'd met her several times already, the last occasion being a family gathering at Christmas, and we'd got on well.

The authentic tones of south-east England greeted me over the phone when I rang her up.

'Matilda, how nice to hear from you. That's more than I can say for that son of mine and you can tell him I said so.'

'He's rather up to his neck at the moment,' I said rather awkwardly. 'You must have heard about Marie-Paule?'

'Yes, I did,' Maggie said grimly. 'And although I don't want to speak ill of the dead, I have to say that I'm not in the least surprised. I can think of about half a dozen people down here who'd like to have done it themselves. Who did do it, by the way?'

'The police don't know yet. Listen, I'm coming down to Lier tomorrow for a couple of days on business and I'd like to see you. Can you spare me an hour or two?'

'Of course I can. Where are you staying?'

'I haven't got anything arranged yet, but—'

'Oh good!' Maggie said instantly. 'Come and stay here. It'll be nice to have some company and we can have a good old gossip. How about it? I'll have lunch ready for you tomorrow at twelve-thirty. Happy hour at twelve.'

I had to laugh. Maggie was incorrigible.

'Lovely,' I said. 'See you then.'

Was I going to tell her Luc and I had split up? I debated the point all down the motorway on Monday morning and still hadn't made my mind up when I reached Lier's mediaeval walls. It's a pretty town, with ramparts, peaceful canals and old almshouses, but I had no eyes for its attractions today. I parked in front of Maggie's red brick bungalow and got out. She was in the garden, studying something on the ground.

'Do you know anything about gardening?' she asked me without preamble. 'Do you think this is dead or not?'

I studied the unpromising-looking piece of plant-life and was unable to pronounce.

'I suppose I'd better leave it in,' she said, reaching up and giving me a quick kiss on the cheek. 'I think the frost got it, but you never know. Come in.'

Maggie was small, blonde and eccentric. Forty years in Flanders hadn't changed her Englishness one bit. We might have been in Petts Wood. I looked round the bungalow and asked, 'Haven't you ever thought of going back to the UK?'

'Whatever for?' she replied, handing me a double sherry. 'I've got my friends and my family here, and a nice little social life: bridge, the choral society, my voluntary work. And England's so depressing these days, what with everybody agonizing over the Common Market and the pound worth about tuppence-halfpenny. Now tell me all about the murder. I went to the funeral, of course, but Luc wasn't exactly forthcoming and we couldn't really talk about it at the graveside, after all.'

This was difficult. How was I going to give her the details without letting on that her son was one of the chief suspects? I did my best, but when I'd finished, Maggie looked at me shrewdly for a moment and said: 'Who do the police think did it?'

'It seems to be a toss-up between the mystery lover, Olivier and Luc,' I said.

'Surely they don't think Luc was involved?' Maggie said, alarmed.

'He doesn't have an alibi. And he had an argument with Marie-Paule a few days before. The divorce would have cleaned him out. And he can't produce his gun for the forensic people.'

In fact, I thought to myself, the circumstantial evidence seemed to be stacking up rather alarmingly.

'Well, where was he?' Maggie asked, going right to the heart of the problem.

'I don't know. He won't tell me.'

'You don't suppose—' she said and then broke off. Then she said, 'No, he wouldn't. Surely?'

'What?'

'He isn't seeing somebody else, is he?'

I sat with my mouth open. I have to admit that it hadn't occurred to me. It would certainly explain a lot of things. Maggie took a look at my face, finished up what was left in her sherry glass and said, 'Let's eat. The casserole's ready.'

She poured me out a generous glass of red wine. My stomach was still reeling from the sherry, but Maggie had spent a lifetime building up an immunity. As she served up the casserole, she said, 'That was a silly thing to say. I'm sorry. I suppose I'm grasping at straws.'

'No, it's a possibility,' I said, rather grimly. 'Given the way things are at the moment.'

Maggie stopped, ladle raised, her face a picture of regret and sympathy. 'Trouble?'

I nodded. 'I think it's over,' I said. 'I hope you don't

61

think I've come down under false pretences.'

'Don't be daft,' she said, resuming her ladling. 'We can be friends, can't we, no matter what that idiotic son of mine does. But I'm so sorry, Matilda. I was really hoping the two of you would make a go of it. Luc needs somebody like you.'

Maybe, I thought glumly, but do I need somebody like him?

'Well, no matter what our personal situation is, I don't think he did it,' I said aloud. 'What's more, I don't think he can have been seeing another woman. There'd have been no reason to hide it from the police. And it was a man who called on Sunday morning. So don't start worrying yet. As I said, the police have got at least two other suspects.'

Maggie snorted. 'They surely can't think it was Olivier? He couldn't kill an ant. Soft as butter.'

'No, my money's on the lover. But it's actually about Olivier I've come down. Did you know that he tried to get custody of Daniel and it turns out that he isn't Daniel's father at all?'

'No, I certainly didn't,' Maggie said, staring. 'Don't tell me that Luc's the child's father after all?'

'No. Father unknown. But Daniel wants to know, so he's asked me to try and track his father down. I thought you could fill me in on the family history. You knew Marie-Paule back then. Did she have anybody else on the string?'

'Knowing her, it's quite likely,' said Maggie trenchantly. 'I always knew she was a cow, and now it's all coming out into the open. Poor Agnès. She's had a miserable life, what with a daughter like that and a tyrant for a husband.'

'That bad?'

Maggie's face puckered. 'Awful! Selfish, intolerant, snobbish, inflexible. I could never stand him. Agnès is a nice woman though. I like her, and she's always had a soft spot for Luc.'

'Well, it looks like Daniel's going to get to stay with them,' I said. The casserole was going down wonderfully. So was the wine. 'He's just got a puppy.'

Maggie snorted again. 'If Agnès wants the legs chewed off her furniture, that's her business,' she said.

Another round of wine splashed into my glass. I thought I'd better get on with the investigation while I still could.

'Where did you first meet Marie-Paule?' I asked.

'At the football club. Luc was in the local team, as you know. There was a match one Christmas and a dance afterwards and she came down from Brussels with another girl who had a boyfriend in the team. She just dazzled everybody. Beautiful, of course, and madly glamorous. She put all the girls' noses out of joint and the men all fell like ninepins.'

'Including Luc,' I said. I could just imagine it.

Maggie nodded sadly. 'He hadn't had a really serious girlfriend before. There'd been a couple of girls at university, and then he did his military service and joined the gendarmerie. Marie-Paule just bowled him over, and nobody knew she was seeing Olivier at the same time. Olivier was in the team too. His wife was pregnant with their first child – they'd only been married a few months.'

'What's his wife like?' I asked, curious.

'Sabine? Wet as a scrubbed hammock,' Maggie said succinctly. 'It was an arranged marriage – the families knew each other.' She paused and stared into her wineglass for a moment. 'I never understood what Marie-Paule saw in Olivier – a nice enough chap, but he always reminds me of a spaniel, with those big brown eyes.'

'The trouble with men with dog's eyes,' I said, 'is that you want to kick them. Maybe Marie-Paule liked a man she could dominate.'

'I think she just liked the idea of running them in tandem,' Maggie said bitterly. 'And there was the money, of course. His family's rolling in it. Then when she got pregnant, Luc was the fall-guy. Of course they were at loggerheads after about six weeks. She was such a ruthless woman, you've no idea. If only Luc had had more sense. This may be a Catholic country but she could have gone to England for an abortion, or Holland, and no one would have been the worse off. I always wondered why she didn't. She must have wanted the child very much.'

'So you can't think of anyone else she might have been carrying on with round about the same time?'

Maggie thought hard. 'There was a lot of gossip – you know the way people talk in small towns. But you really ought to ask Luc's cousins. They're all about the same age and they'd know more. They were in the same crowd.'

'How many cousins has he got?'

'Two on the Vanderauwera side,' Maggie said. 'Katrien and Piet. You met Katrien at Christmas. Blonde, skinny, talkative, you remember? She's your best bet. She and Luc were very close as children. She's a teacher at the local school. You haven't met Piet before; he might be worth talking to, but you'll probably think he's a bit odd. And then there's Brigitte Giestelinck; she's a second cousin, but she used to hang about with Luc's crowd too. She's a nurse, looks after her old parents. I think she was at that Christmas party too.'

I was feeling warm and rather relaxed. Maggie got up to open another bottle.

'Tell you what,' she said, pouring. 'The bird protection society's got an evening tonight, and Katrien'll be there – she's a leading light. We'll go along and corner her. Then you can talk to Piet and Brigitte tomorrow. Piet doesn't work and hardly ever goes out of the house, so he's easy. We'll call Brigitte this evening and fix a time to go and see her.'

'OK,' I said. My elbow was having trouble staying on the table. Maggie was slightly pink.

She looked at me rather glassily for a long moment and then said, 'We all hated Marie-Paule, you know. She was such a – a destroyer. That's what she was. She didn't care what she did as long as she got what she wanted. I could have killed her for what she did to Luc.'

'Don't tell the police that,' I said.

Maggie shrugged. 'I don't care. It seems like justice, you know. It's awful and I know I shouldn't say it, but I'm glad she's dead. How about some dessert?'

Chapter Nine

We took a long nap after lunch. Maggie woke me up with tea and biscuits at five. I had trouble keeping my eyes open, but a brisk walk in the cold winter air fixed that. As I came back in, Maggie said, 'I'll call Brigitte and see when she's free.'

'Maggie, I'd rather you didn't mention to anyone about Luc and me splitting up,' I said, rather awkwardly. 'I don't think I could face having to explain it all just yet. Do you mind?'

'Of course not. I quite understand,' Maggie said, dialling busily.

The appointment was made for four the next day, after the usual exchange of enquiries about health and comments about the weather.

'That's done,' Maggie said, putting the phone down. 'Now for the bird-lovers. There's a couple of short films followed by refreshments, so with a bit of luck we won't have to cook supper.'

The thought of supper did nothing for me at all. I was still stuffed full of lunch. I had some qualms about my blood alcohol levels, but the gathering was within walking distance, in a local cultural centre, an unadorned red-brick building which reminded me of my old school. There was a sizeable crowd. They were definitely not the beautiful people; in fact, the anorak-and-welly brigade seemed to be represented in large numbers. The films were in Flemish and quite fascinating: one about falcons nesting in Paris and the other about reintroducing vultures into the Causses. I enjoyed them. I thought involuntarily of Marius Charpentier. His face would have fitted in this kind of crowd. A pleasant-looking man with a beard told us about breeding successes among rare birds of prey, and everybody clapped, including me.

Maggie grabbed my arm. 'There's Katrien,' she hissed, pointing down towards the stage. 'Front row, third from right.'

I saw a head of curly blonde hair and a sharp profile with a pair of large specs slipping down the nose. The lights came up and everybody stood up, some people still applauding.

'Come on,' Maggie said and set off determinedly through the swathes of people. Katrien was talking to a hook-nosed man who looked like a large bird of prey himself, but she greeted Maggie with a big smile and kissed her enthusiastically before turning to me. 'Of course I remember you,' she said to me. Her English was excellent. 'It's so nice to see you again. How's Luc?'

'Fine,' I said, carefully not looking at Maggie, who wasn't looking at me.

'Matilda's doing some investigation—' Maggie began, but Katrien interrupted before she could finish ' – About Marie-Paule? I'm dying to hear the details. Let's go and get a drink. Come on, this way. We'd better hurry or there'll be none left.'

In the foyer, jammed elbow to elbow in the crowd, an unwanted sandwich in one hand and an unwanted glass of orange juice in the other, I began, 'It's not actually about the murder—'

'What a terrible thing!' Katrien exclaimed, pushing her specs up her nose. 'Whoever could have done it? Well, that's a stupid question, because half the people in Lier could have done it.'

'Exactly what I said,' Maggie said. 'But that's not really what—'

'How's Luc taking it?' Katrien demanded, fixing me with anxious blue eyes.

'Not too bad,' I said. 'Would you mind—'

'And the poor little boy,' Katrien said, shaking her head. 'It's always the children that suffer most, of course. Is he staying with his grandparents?'

I opened my mouth, but wasn't quite quick enough.

'Much the best thing for him, of course,' Katrien said. 'A stable environment's what children need, don't you agree?'

'Katrien, will you listen for a minute?' Maggie said exasperatedly. 'And people accuse me of being talkative! Matilda wants to ask you something.'

Katrien gave the specs another shove and looked at me expectantly through them. I opened my mouth again, and Maggie said, 'We want to know if Marie-Paule was seeing anybody else round about the time she and Luc got involved. Apart from Olivier and Luc, that is.'

I closed my mouth. These Vanderauweras were hard to compete with.

'You mean sleeping with,' Katrien said. 'Why?'

'Because Daniel wants to find out who his father is and it isn't either Luc or Olivier.'

'How do they know?' Katrien asked, her eyes huge.

Now or never. Jump, Matilda, quick.

'Medical tests,' I said. 'Any ideas?'

'Well, there was a persistent rumour that she'd had a fling with the football team coach,' Katrien said slowly. 'But it couldn't have lasted long. He was an ex-professional from Sweden and he went back a couple of weeks after Christmas.'

'Once is all it takes,' Maggie said grimly. 'What was his name?'

'Anders somebody . . . I can't remember. Ring the football club – they'll be able to tell you. But you know, Matilda, it wasn't necessarily somebody from Lier.

Heaven knows what she was getting up to in Brussels. She had her own flat, and a job – the possibilities were endless.'

'What did she do?'

'She worked for a PR agency. I don't know the name.'

'Let's think a minute,' Maggie said, frowning. 'Luc and Marie-Paule were married in March. Daniel was born mid-August. That means he must have been conceived before she ever came here – in November some time. Katrien's right – it's more likely to have happened in Brussels.'

'There was no question of a premature birth?' I asked.

They both shook their heads firmly.

'He was a huge baby,' Maggie said. 'Embarrassingly so, under the circumstances.'

'You should talk to Piet,' Katrien said, staring at me anxiously. 'He hung around with the lads on the team and you might get some of the locker-room gossip.'

'We thought we'd have a word with Brigitte too,' Maggie said.

Katrien grimaced. 'Oh, Brigitte! Well, I suppose you might get something out of her. She was always trailing around after Luc in those days. She's a great admirer of yours, incidentally, Matilda.'

'Of mine?' I asked, startled.

'Oh, yes. Ever since that Christmas party. She keeps saying how glad she is Luc's found somebody decent at last.'

I felt myself going warm about the cheeks.

'She ought to go out and find somebody herself,' Maggie said, faint exasperation in her voice.

'She says her parents would never cope without her,' Katrien told us.

'Rubbish! They'd be a lot happier not being ordered about every minute of the day. She should get out, buy some new clothes and have a little fun.'

'That's what I keep saying to Piet, too,' Katrien said.

'But he's as deaf as a post when he wants to be. Honestly, Maggie, families are the end!'

'You don't have to tell me,' Maggie said with feeling.

This looked like it was going to degenerate into a family griping session, but luckily the bird-man appeared out of the crowd and grabbed Katrien's arm with a hissed enquiry about the projector, and off she whizzed. I put my glass down thankfully; orange juice always gives me heartburn. We didn't stay long. I was glad to get out of the heat and the deafening Flemish noise.

'So what's Piet's problem?' I asked Maggie as we made our way home through the dark streets.

'He won the Lotto,' Maggie said, exasperation in her voice again.

'That's a problem?' I asked. I could do with a problem like that.

'Well, no, but now he won't go out to work. He gave up his job and sits at home all day doing nothing. My sister-in-law's in despair. She can't get rid of him. If he were my son, I'd throw him out of the house.'

I thought about that somewhat reflectively when I met Piet next day. He was hugely fat; his shirt buttons were strained to their limits over a vast belly, while his trousers, bought to fit the maximum circumference, hung down baggily in the seat and resembled nothing so much as an armchair cover. He was a tall man and moved with ponderous deliberation. The rather small head that sat atop the pear-shaped body was oval and smooth, with wisps of untidy brown hair on the cranium. His expression was mild and rather pleasant; small grey eyes studied me calmly. I had a moment's wild hilarity at the idea of Maggie throwing him anywhere.

I'd been shown into his room by his mother, a large, bustling lady known to the whole family as Tante Lieve. She was Maggie's sister-in-law. The house was large and dim, decorated in best Belgian style with appalling floral wallpaper and enormous dark furniture. Mother-in-

70

Laws' Tongues stood on all the window-sills, their spiked blades entangled in the net curtains. It was hideous.

'Mother, can you bring some coffee?' Piet called, as Tante Lieve closed the door. Then he smiled at me and held out a large pink paw.

'I've heard about you,' he said. 'I'm very glad to meet you. How's Luc?'

Most educated Flemish people speak English and he was no exception. I muttered something non-committal about Luc and sat down in the chair indicated. Piet lowered himself into a vast, solid armchair and said with a twinkle, 'I expect they've warned you about me, have they? Piet the lazy one, who sits at home all day doing nothing?'

'They're all jealous,' I said, looking at the chair legs and wondering about stress factors. 'What did you do before?'

'I was working in the Ministry of Finance,' he said solemnly.

'Well, no wonder you wanted to give it up!' I exclaimed.

Piet laughed. 'You understand,' he said. 'Ten years doing the same job, in the same office, with the same people and the same pitiful salary. No hope of promotion or payrises. The same trip into work each day at the same time and the same trip home in the evening. It's enough to drive anybody mad. Now I can get up when I want, come and go as I please, and if I don't want to do anything at all, it's OK. Paradise.'

The door opened and Tante Lieve came in with a loaded tray. Coffee and cake. I'd just had breakfast. She put the tray down, fussed over it for a minute or two, and went out again, with a fond look at her son. Another devoted mother.

'Katrien rang me,' Piet said, handing me a vast slice of cake. 'You're trying to find out who Daniel's father might have been?'

'Any ideas?' I asked.

'To be honest, no. Though from what transpired later, it might have been anyone. We didn't find out what she was really like till after she and Luc got married.'

'Katrien said there was gossip.'

'Yes, a little, but we gave her the benefit of the doubt at first. There was no real evidence. The girls were all wild because Marie-Paule was so stunning. And the men couldn't see past her.'

'Including you?' I asked, looking at him keenly.

He smiled. 'I was eighteen and very impressionable,' he said. 'And she was very charming in those days, even to fat, unprepossessing young men like me. Once she'd hooked Luc, of course, that all changed. She made it very clear that I was beneath her notice.'

'You disliked her?'

He paused for a long moment, looking into space.

'I was afraid of her,' he said finally, surprising me. 'She was completely ruthless. She used everybody. So I just stayed away from her. I haven't seen her for years.'

'Did she and Luc start going out together immediately?'

'Pretty much. Luc was very – competitive. In many ways, they were well matched.'

No one had said this in so many words before. I looked at Piet thoughtfully.

'How do you mean?'

'They were both clever, ambitious, full of confidence in themselves, self-willed, determined.' He stopped and looked me full in the face. 'But you must know this,' he said gently. 'You know Luc.'

I didn't want to have to admit it. Instead I said, 'Why did he agree to marry her? Luc hates being pressured.'

'To be fair, he felt a sense of duty. And he was really infatuated with her. And also, as you know, her father was highly placed in the police-force. It was a huge boost for Luc's career. As I said, he was very ambitious.'

Unflattering as it might be to Luc, it had an uncomfortably plausible ring. Avoiding the mild brown eyes, I said, 'Did anybody know about the affair with Olivier?'

'Not a soul. He'd only been married a little while. Of course, it was a *mariage d'intérêt*, but then Sabine turned out to be expecting and Olivier's father decided to send him to Zaire to run the family firm there.'

'So if Olivier was her first choice,' I said, half to myself, 'she soon found out that she was barking up the wrong tree.'

If I was right, Marie-Paule had known she was pregnant when she first came to Lier. She was looking for a father for her baby. Olivier was the first choice: adoring, rich and manageable. When that turned out to be impossible, she'd settled for Luc. But she'd told both men that they were Daniel's father.

'But why,' I said, thinking out loud, 'didn't she marry Daniel's real father?'

'Who knows?' Piet said, shrugging. 'Maybe he'd abandoned her. Maybe he was already married.'

I sighed.

'You don't happen to know anything about her life in Brussels, do you?' I asked.

'Not much. She worked for a firm called Cornavin SA – public relations or advertising or something like that. Brigitte can probably tell you more. She was quite good friends with the other girl, Nicole, the one who brought Marie-Paule down here in the first place.'

So Lier looked like a dead end. Brussels was the place I should be looking. I just hoped Brigitte would be able to give me something useful. Otherwise my only other source of information was Marie-Paule's mother, and I could hardly go there and ask for information about her deceased daughter's sex-life.

Chapter Ten

Maggie came with me to see Brigitte that afternoon. I had no recollection of meeting Brigitte before, but the square-faced, short-haired, plain woman who opened the door with a friendly smile did look rather familiar. She had a firm handshake and a no-nonsense manner. Her dark sensible clothes reinforced the impression of the competent district nurse. We were taken into the sitting-room and introduced to two pale silent elderly people; then Brigitte ushered us into her own office. She worked from home, though as she explained, she was attached to a local clinic specializing in geriatric care.

We were served yet more coffee and cakes, as it was mid-afternoon. My heart sank, but we couldn't refuse. I'd just have to go on a diet when I got home. Brigitte listened interestedly to my explanation of the situation.

'I remember it all very well,' she said, when I'd finished. We were speaking French, as Brigitte's English, unlike that of her cousins, was rather poor. 'I had my doubts about Marie-Paule from the beginning, but none of the men could see through her. And by the time she'd got her claws into Luc, it was too late. And then, of course, when Daniel was born . . . well, anyone can count to nine, can't they?'

'What I really need is information about her life in Brussels before she ever came here, and Piet said you knew her friend, Nicole.'

'Well, I didn't know her very well,' Brigitte said, rather

doubtfully. 'She was working in the same office as Marie-Paule. She only came down here half a dozen times. But I met her in Brussels a couple of years later when I was up on a training course and we had lunch together.'

'What was her surname?'

Brigitte frowned, thinking. 'De Becker. Something like that. But she's probably married by now.'

'And she was working for Cornavin too?'

'Yes, that was the name, but she wasn't working there any more. Marie-Paule had had her fired.'

'What? Why?'

'Well, Marie-Paule kept on with her job after she got married, and when she came back from pregnancy leave, she got herself promoted to a management position. Nicole said it was because she had the managing director in her pocket. There was a row and Marie-Paule had her dismissed.'

'Do you know the managing director's name?'

Brigitte shook her head.

From the corner by the window where she was sitting, Maggie remarked in inimitably Petts Wood French: 'Somebody else with a possible motive?'

Brigitte looked up. 'For killing Marie-Paule, you mean? Not after all this time, surely?'

'Marie-Paule had a gift for getting herself hated,' I said grimly.

'Yes,' Brigitte said simply. 'I hadn't seen her for several years, but I don't suppose she'd changed. Have the police made any progress?'

I shook my head. 'They have a number of suspects,' I said.

'Including Olivier and Luc,' Maggie added.

'Luc!' Brigitte exclaimed. 'That's ridiculous. Surely they don't think Luc did it?'

A little colour had suddenly come into her rather doughy cheeks. She wore no make-up at all and the grey light wasn't kind to her skin.

'I'm sure they'll find the real culprit soon,' Maggie said

75

in a rallying tone. 'Don't you worry about it, Brigitte. By the way, how did you get on with that gynaecologist I recommended? Did she sort you out?'

The abrupt change of subject told me suddenly just how edgy Maggie was about Luc's possible involvement. It didn't reassure me. Brigitte didn't seem to notice, though. Her colour faded and she smiled.

'Oh, yes,' she said. 'I'm having a course of treatment and it seems to be working at last.'

'Oh good,' Maggie said, rather distractedly. She'd begun to fidget.

There wasn't much more to be learned here. I got up and held out my hand.

'Thanks very much for your help,' I said.

'It's a pleasure,' Brigitte said warmly, getting up too. 'I really wanted to meet you again. I can't say how pleased I am that Luc's found somebody like you – you're exactly what he needs. I thought so the minute I first saw you.'

Embarrassment effectively wiped out the details of leave-taking from my memory. Back in the car, I said, 'I wish people wouldn't keep saying things like that. I don't know where to put myself.'

'It is awkward,' Maggie agreed. A moment later she added, 'Brigitte does annoy me. I don't know why.'

I was surprised. Brigitte had seemed very straightforward and helpful. I said as much.

'I know, I know,' Maggie said with a sigh. 'She's competent and hard-working and infinitely patient with all those elderly people, and a pillar of the community and all that. She just gets up my nose, that's all.'

There was a short silence. Then Maggie added, 'All the same, she's got her oddities. She's paranoid about dirt – keeps the house spotless. And she's got a positive phobia about insects and mice and things.'

I smiled. 'All nurses are paranoid about dirt. I had a great-aunt who'd been a hospital matron and everybody coming into the house got sprayed with disinfectant, including the dog.'

'I suppose we're all peculiar in our own way,' Maggie said.

No comment.

So all in all, Lier had been unproductive, apart from a couple of extra kilos round the Plimsoll line. At home, Hortense was still sneezing and the agency was still unable to provide me with employment. There was a postcard from the bank, asking me to contact them. I put it in the garbage. I wanted to know how the enquiry was getting on, but had no means of finding out, short of ringing up the police and asking them. I wondered if Marius Charpentier knew anything and tried to call him, but had to be satisfied with leaving a message on his answer-phone. There was no sign of life from Luc; I didn't know whether to be glad or sorry.

The trip to Lier mightn't have helped much in the matter of Daniel's father, but it had shed much light on places which had hitherto been obscure. I wasn't sure if that was a good thing, but you can't put the genie back in the lamp. Up till then, Luc had been Marie-Paule's innocent victim in my mind; now Piet's comments had put him in a much less flattering light. Knowing Luc as I did, I could well believe that ambition had played a large part in the whole affair.

When the first scale falls from your eyes, the rest follow rather rapidly. In spite of my indignant denials concerning Luc's involvement in the murder, I couldn't rid my mind of a number of nagging doubts. Why lie about his gun? Why couldn't he provide an alibi for the time of the murder? And if it came to that, where had he been when Daniel had had his accident? Where had the new jacket and all that money come from? And what about the trip to Poland?

I don't believe in coincidences. It all had to be connected somehow.

Next stop, Antwerp!

Chapter Eleven

Antwerp was the next destination in the magical mystery tour.

Antwerp's very different to Brussels. It has the saltiness and crude energy of a major port, combined with stubborn Flemish independence and the eternal desire of all second cities to cock a snook at the capital. It has great shopping. It has a terrific zoo. It has Rubens. It's an invigorating place to visit, and not just because of the sea air.

They were digging up the roads that day, and the traffic was being funnelled off in all directions by little orange signs bearing the magic word '*Wegomlegging*', which has got 'Abracadabra' beat in all ways as far as I'm concerned.

Consequently I got lost and took a while to find the garage I was looking for. It turned out to be a combination car workshop and van-hire firm in a rather dusty back-street. Two dirty white vans were parked against the kerb, the name of the firm on their sides almost obscured by dust. The workshop door was wide open and the repair-pit gaped wide in the floor. The place was deserted. A door to one side bore a sign which said: '*Kantoor*'.

Be bold, Matilda. I rapped smartly and strode in. A small plain office with a cheap metal desk and filing cabinet. An old typewriter on a side-table. Two battered chairs. Papers scattered about and a trade calendar on the wall. Another door with an opaque glass panel and a sign saying '*Uitgang*'.

There was nobody there. It was only eleven in the morning; they couldn't possibly be at lunch yet. A faint smell of cheap perfume hung about the room.

It took me three minutes to examine the papers. All were in Flemish and appeared to be standard business documents: invoices, credit notes, estimates for repairs, time-sheets. A small grey notebook turned out to be a van-hire log-book; they weren't doing very good business. A couple of assignments a day, not enough to stay afloat in these rocky times. Perhaps the garage was doing better. I had a quick look in the filing cabinet. The drawers were wonky and the whole cabinet rocked as I pulled them out one after another. Customer files, supplier files, etcetera. All the accounts books were stacked casually on top of the cabinet. I gave them the once-over; the company wouldn't have won any prizes for book-keeping. In fact, the whole set-up had an oddly cursory air, as if it were on the verge of bankruptcy and nobody cared any more.

I wanted to talk to someone. Pulling open the back door, I found myself in a large enclosed courtyard with a few cars parked in it. Buildings surrounded it; many of the windows were broken or boarded up. Across the yard was a low concrete building which looked like a garage; the entrance stood open, rubber folding doors pulled back. I made my way cautiously across and peered in. I could hear the faint hum of noise and voices from somewhere. There were greasy tyre-marks on the concrete floor, leading towards another garage entrance inside, firmly closed. To my left was an orange-painted door with an elbow-shaped closing-mechanism at the top. I pulled it open with difficulty, and went down a flight of concrete steps to another similar door at the bottom. Both doors were marked '*Geen toegang*' but neither was locked. The noise was louder here. I pulled the second door open and stepped in.

79

I once saw a production of *Rheingold* in which Nibelheim looked like an East German car-factory, with the dwarfs scampering about in the gloom among the half-built carcasses of cheap cars. This was just like it. It was crowded and dark, except for the flare of welding torches here and there and pools of light where people were working. There must have been half a dozen cars being repaired. The clang of tools on metal reinforced the Nibelheim effect. Nobody was singing, though.

My luck ran out then. As I stood gaping, the door behind me was yanked open and a voice said roughly, '*God verdomme!*'

There were three men and none of them looked friendly. Two were dressed in dirty overalls and needed baths. The third was in casual clothes, with a square reptilian face and heavily greased hair.

Like a good boy scout, I had a story all prepared. Grasping my handbag firmly, I smiled, put on my best Celia Johnson accent and said politely, with exaggerated enunciation: 'Do you speak English? *English?* Do you speak ENGLISH?'

Celia Johnson would have got a better reception. A large filthy hand seized my arm and yanked me brutally out of the workshop. I found myself pinned up against the cement wall, one man holding each arm, while the reptile ripped my handbag from my shoulder and upended it on the floor.

I stopped being Celia Johnson rather suddenly and became Matilda Haycastle again.

'What the hell do you think you're doing?' I began furiously, but for all the notice they took, I needn't have bothered. I tugged angrily at the restraining arms and was yanked back against the wall so hard I bumped my head. What was all this about?

The reptile had found my wallet and was studying my ID card. Without glancing up, he snapped something in Flemish. My two captors hesitated and looked at one another uncertainly. The order came again like a whip-lash. Tentative, embarrassed hands groped in my pockets. I struggled again, uselessly. One of the men said, '*Niets.*'

The reptile looked up at me now, and something in his expression made me realize that I might have made a rather dangerous mistake. In guttural, but understandable English, he said, 'Who are you? What do you want?'

Luckily, I remembered my story.

'Luc Vanderauwera sent me. He's my friend. He was working for you a couple of weeks ago and he lost his credit cards and he asked me to come and find them for him. They must be here somewhere. We've looked everywhere else. Did anybody find a small wallet with half a dozen cards in it? Black leather, you know the type of thing?'

Nervousness made me garrulous. I rabbited on, while the expression on the two mechanics' faces turned slowly from suspicion to bewilderment. The reptile was watching me closely. As I came to a faltering stop, he said, 'Credit cards?'

'Yes, you know, American Express, Visa, that kind of thing.'

Up above, I heard the sound of the upper door opening. The reptile's face assumed what might possibly have been the beginning of a smile.

'We shall see,' he said. He turned and called, '*Kom beneden!*'

Two pairs of legs appeared at the top of my field of vision, descending. One pair was shapely, feminine and stockinged, ending in unsuitably frivolous high-heeled shoes. The other pair belonged to Luc.

This was definitely not my lucky day. It hadn't even occurred to me that he might be here. He looked as flabbergasted to see me as I was to see him. My brain revolved uselessly, like an engine with an overstretched fan-belt. The girl beside him was blonde, about twenty-

81

two, pretty in an unintelligent sort of way, made-up, mini-skirted. She was wearing the same over-sweet perfume that had been hanging about the office.

It was Maggie who saved me, indirectly. At least, it was a comment Maggie had made. I leapt into action before my brain had even finished formulating what to do. Lurching forward, I said, injecting as much contempt, anger and jealousy into my voice as I could, 'So I've caught you out at last. This is what you get up to when you tell me you're working! What do you think I am, stupid? I know when you're lying to me. Up in Antwerp doing a bit of work, my foot. This is what you bloody well come up to Antwerp for, isn't it?'

And leaping forward from the loosened grip of my captors, I charged up the steps and seized the unfortunate girl's arm. Alarm and bewilderment invested the rather plump face, but I couldn't spare a thought for her feelings. Pushing her out of the way, I screamed into Luc's face, 'This is the *last bloody time* you get away with it, do you hear me? I'm not going to go on taking this kind of treatment. I just won't stand for it.'

I'll say this for Luc, he was always quick on the uptake. Even before the echoes of my fishwife screaming had died away, he'd picked me up and was yelling right back.

'You stupid jealous cow, I've just about had enough of you. I can't go anywhere without you following me about like a goddamned bloodhound. You're paranoid, Matilda. It wouldn't bloody well be surprising if I did want to screw everything in sight, would it? I'm sick of it. Get off my bloody back or I'll really give you what for.'

He sounded so convincing and looked so furious that I took an involuntary step back down, tears coming into my eyes. Luc followed me down, his face dangerous, his hand raised. For a moment I really thought he was going to clout me.

'What the hell's going on?' said the reptile, tiredly.

A burst of angry Flemish followed. I was wildly jealous, I was always making trouble about other women, he was sick to death of me, he was going to take me home and give me a good hiding. I could tell they believed us; the tension had gone completely out of the situation. Thank heaven, because I'd reached my limit. I couldn't have thought up another lie if my life depended on it. Luckily, I didn't need to. Still spitting out angry Flemish, Luc seized my handbag, shovelled all my bits and pieces into it and stuffed it into my hands. Then he grabbed my arm in a painful grip and hustled me unceremoniously up the steps, through the yard and back out into the street.

My hands were trembling so much I couldn't drive and Luc had to take the wheel. His face was grim. He drove to Antwerp station in silence and parked the car. Then he leant his arms on the wheel, and slowly bent his head till his forehead rested on them. We said nothing for a long time. In the distance, faintly, I could hear the lions roaring in the zoo behind the station.

Luc broke the silence first.

'Christ, Matilda,' he said wearily, 'you like living dangerously, don't you?'

I swallowed and searched for my voice. 'Thanks,' I said, with difficulty. 'I owe you one.'

He lifted his head then, and the flicker of a tired smile appeared.

'Don't mention it,' he said. 'How did you find out where the garage was?'

'You left a business card in the flat.'

'Oh,' Luc said. 'I should have known better. That was one hell of a lucky escape. Those people aren't fooling around. You might have ended up in the harbour in a cement overcoat.'

A measure of intimacy had returned between us, no doubt due to the shared danger. It was the last flicker of a dying flame. I looked directly at my ex-lover and said, 'What's it all about? I won't tell the police. Not after this.'

He didn't answer for a long while and I thought he

wasn't going to. Then he said, rather wearily, 'The garage recycles stolen cars for export to the East. They needed people to drive them to Poland. From there they get taken on into Russia and sold.'

'You were driving a stolen car to Poland when Daniel had his accident?' I exclaimed, shocked.

Luc nodded. 'The money was good,' he said. 'Very good. I needed all the extra cash I could get, but it had to be in the black otherwise Marie-Paule might have got her hands on it. Not to mention the tax people.'

'I could have lent you money,' I said, still shocked. 'You didn't need to commit a crime.'

'Not that kind of money,' Luc said, with that half-smile again.

'But what did you need it for?' I exclaimed.

'I was planning to go to the US,' he said. 'I spent some time over there when I was in the police and I've got a few contacts. And I like America. It was a chance of making a new start.' After a moment, he added, 'I was going to ask you to come, too. Before all this happened.'

While I was still digesting this, he added, 'I sold my gun in Warsaw. They pay good money on the black market.'

'And the Sunday Marie-Paule was killed?'

'I was here in Antwerp making arrangements for another trip.'

'I see,' I said. 'What happens if the police find out about the cars?'

'With my record? Prison,' he said. 'Only that's not going to happen if I can help it. The operation's going underground immediately. That's why I came up today, to help organize it.'

'But you'll have to tell Roland eventually,' I protested. 'You're one of the suspects in the murder case. Suppose they arrest you?'

'They can't, they haven't got any real evidence. Anyway, they'll have to find me first.'

I looked at him sharply. 'What are you planning?'

'Matilda, what you don't know won't hurt you. If they ask, you can say you last saw me in Antwerp. That's all.'

'But if you disappear, it'll look like you're guilty,' I protested, rather forlornly. I knew what Luc was like with his mind made up. I looked at the rakish profile above the upturned jacket collar and, depressingly, felt not a flicker of lust. After a moment, I added, 'Who do you think killed her?'

'I haven't the faintest idea,' Luc said. 'Anyone could have done it. The maid. Olivier. The mystery visitor. Or somebody we know nothing about. The enquiry's stuck till they find the murder weapon, or that young man turns up.'

'Somebody'd better unstick it, then,' I said.

Luc turned to look at me. 'Go ahead,' he said. 'If ever there was a time to use your talents, this is it.'

'While you're here—' I said.

Luc groaned. 'I said I should have known better. OK, what is it? But make it snappy. I've got to go.'

'Do you have any idea who Daniel's father might have been? Anyone Marie-Paule was seeing when you first knew her.'

'No,' he said, extremely shortly. 'I don't.'

He turned and made as if to open the car door.

I said, 'I wouldn't have come. To the US, I mean.'

He looked back at me, his dark blue eyes serious. 'No, I didn't think you would.'

He hesitated for a moment, then leaning over, he kissed my cheek and said, 'Goodbye, Matilda. Good luck.'

I watched him walk purposefully into the station entrance and disappear into the darkness. There was something final about it, but I didn't feel particularly sad. It seemed a more fitting ending than the shouting match we'd had in the flat. I don't like things to finish on a bitter note.

Chapter Twelve

Maybe I should get an answering machine. It seemed like the whole of Brussels had been trying to get hold of me while I was away, because the phone didn't stop ringing once I was home. The agency with a job for next week, Alleluiah. My bank, politely concerned about my overdraft and did I perhaps wish to talk to them about a temporary loan to tide me over, at very reasonable rates? Reasonable for them, anyway. Marius Charpentier, to tell me he'd prepared a list of contacts working in the drugs field and he was going to send it to me. Daniel, enquiring about my progress.

'Have you found him yet?'

'Daniel, it's only been five days,' I said, my voice rising slightly. 'This is going to take some time.'

'Will you have found out anything by the time I get back from the mountains?'

'When will that be?'

'I'm leaving tomorrow. We're going for ten days.'

'Maybe,' I said. 'Tell you what, why don't you come to tea when you get back? I'll introduce you to Hortense.'

'All right,' Daniel said enthusiastically. 'I'll call you when I get back.'

I put the phone down with a wry face. The universe is black and white to children. I was going to have to come up with a result, or risk disappointing Daniel beyond measure. For a fleeting moment, I wished I hadn't got myself into this. I made a mental note to tell Daniel not to bring Daisy when he came for tea; Hortense would have her on toast.

My attention was rapidly distracted, when the phone rang again and I found myself talking to Agnès Gheyssens. Could she come and see me? There was something she wanted to discuss. Of course, I said. When? This afternoon. She must have been phoning from the corner café, because I'd hardly had time to put the sitting-room in order before the doorbell rang. She was beautifully dressed, with a round fur hat and neat gloves, and she carried an expensive umbrella, but her face was white under the fur and two patches of uneven rouge showed on her cheeks.

I offered refreshment and she refused. She sat, twisting her gloves in her lap, and said, 'Daniel has told me that he's asked you to find his father.'

'Yes,' I said. There really wasn't anything else I could say.

'I came to ask you if – if you could find a way to – to disappoint him.'

I let the silence stretch out, then said, gently, 'Why?'

'My husband is – not very well,' she said, her dark eyes wretched. 'The police have told us – they have evidence that – that our daughter was – promiscuous.'

'But they told me they were going to keep that confidential!' I exclaimed, shocked.

She smiled rather wanly. 'Did they?' she said. 'Well, they told us. Pierre refused to believe it at first. He thought that the maid must be lying. But there's too much evidence – too many witnesses. In the end he had to accept it. He hasn't been himself since. If – if you find out any more, it'll only make it worse.'

I was still shocked by the perfidy of the police and had to pull myself together to answer her. 'I think it's very important to Daniel, or I wouldn't have agreed to do it,' I said. 'He's just lost his mother and two potential fathers. He needs to know who his parents were. And I've promised. I can't let him down. But if it's any comfort, I have to say that the chances of success are minimal. The trail's too cold.'

She said nothing, but the forlorn dark eyes continued to look at me pleadingly.

'Did you know she was pregnant when she married Luc?' I asked suddenly.

I half expected her to react indignantly, but she didn't. She just said, 'Yes,' on a kind of sob, then she went on in a rush, 'I didn't want them to marry – I thought they were wrong for one another and I didn't see why they should be in such a hurry. So then she told me. She said Luc was the father.'

'And when Daniel was born?'

'We never talked about it,' Agnès said. 'We never discussed those things in our home. I told you, she and I were never close. She was her father's girl, always.'

'Do you have any idea whom she might have been seeing?'

She shook her head slowly. 'She led her own life. The job, the flat. Holidays alone or with girl friends. She never confided in me.'

She had all the unhappy dignity of a desperately lonely woman. I felt terribly sorry for her.

'Madame Gheyssens,' I said, 'I'll do my very best not to stir up any more dirt. That isn't my intention at all. But I really do think Daniel has a right to know. He's had a very rough deal so far. I don't want to let him down too.'

After a long silence, I heard her sigh. She seemed to lose a little of her rigidity.

'I'm sorry,' she said. 'I know I shouldn't have asked you. But I'm so afraid that the truth may just cause more harm. Have you thought of that?'

'Yes,' I said. 'I have. Please trust me.'

'I think I do,' she said, with a shadowy smile. 'Thank you for seeing me, Miss Haycastle.'

After she'd gone, I sat down and put my feet up to think it all over. Hortense, still snuffling, climbed onto my chest and settled down heavily with her head on my shoulder, seeking warmth. I stroked her absently. It seemed to me that the repercussions of Marie-Paule's career and abrupt end were only just starting to make themselves felt. The sheer force of her personality must have been considerable to have held everything together when she was alive. So many people caught and held and used and discarded at will. But why? What was the point of it all? Self-gratification? Security? I'd only met Marie-Paule once, but I certainly hadn't had the impression of a spoiled rich little Daddy's girl. She had been a lioness: a strong, experienced, dangerous hunter. A fighter. There's nothing more deadly, they say, than a lioness defending her cub.

And then, of course, I knew I had the answer. Daniel was the key. Daniel was the reason for it all. She'd set out to give her child a name and a home, and when she couldn't get Olivier, she'd taken Luc instead. Only that had been a mistake, because he was as ruthless as she, in his way. So to get rid of him, she'd told him he wasn't the child's father and demanded a divorce and Luc, out of bitter pride and bloody-mindedness, refused. It had cost them both seven years of misery.

Then I'd arrived on the scene. Good old Matilda Haycastle, always in the right place at the right time. Marie-Paule must have been rubbing her hands with glee. Now she'd get her divorce, and there was Olivier waiting, arms outstretched, adoring, compliant, rich. Never mind the fact that the Delfosse marriage had been smashed to bits. Daniel was safe at last. But then somebody killed her and it had all been for nothing.

She must have loved that child so much.

I was still thinking about it the next day, as I pushed my trolley round the supermarket. In fact I was standing lost in thought in front of the dairy counter when I suddenly had the distinct impression that somebody was watching me. I turned, my sudden movement surprising an elderly lady, who dropped a packet of cheese with a nervous squeak. It was a Saturday afternoon, the worst possible time to go shopping, and there were droves of people. My trolley had a tweezly wheel and was almost unmanageable. I proceeded with difficulty towards the frozen foods, swung round the end of the fridges and disappeared into the biscuits and dry goods, where I stopped and waited. A flash of beige on the edge of my vision made me turn – too late. Attack is the best form of defence, Matilda. Pushing my uncooperative trolley, I whizzed down the alley, narrowly missing a stand of chocolate bars at the end. Nobody. I had to be imagining this. It was a huge supermarket – one could play cat and mouse for ever. I resumed my shopping route, keeping my eyes open. Nothing suspicious at all.

I was squeezing melons in the fruit-and-veg department when a voice said, 'Mademoiselle Haycastle.' It was my turn to jump and squeak; the melon shot out of my hands and hit the floor with a soggy thump.

It was Olivier Delfosse. I stared, shocked. He looked as if he'd been out all night; hair uncombed, chin unshaven, Burberry raincoat crumpled. The brown eyes looked at me miserably. The melon lay unheeded on the floor.

'I've got to talk to you,' he said, almost stammering. He sounded desperate. 'I've been hearing things – about Marie-Paule. All sorts of things. I've got to know if they were true. I thought you would know – is it true? About the – the other men?'

Why was I suddenly the expert on Marie-Paule? Olivier's hands were twitching. Big, solid workman's hands. I said carefully, 'I'm awfully sorry, Monsieur Delfosse. There's no reason to suppose it isn't true.'

'Oh God!' he exclaimed loudly. A couple of people looked at him curiously. He fixed his eyes on me and said, 'I loved her so much. And for so long. I can't believe she's dead. She was so strong, so – so sure. She was always there when I needed her. What am I going to do without her?' And to my utter horror, he began to cry.

I stood rooted to the spot in awe, watching this big man blubber into the avocado pears, his Burberryed shoulders shaking. The crowds of shoppers eddied around us, keeping a safe distance, casting curious glances as they trolleyed past. Three small children stood and stared, frankly interested. You don't get to see grown-ups crying every day.

Girl-Guide training stands one in good stead. Somehow I got Olivier out of the supermarket, and sat him down on a low wall outside. The spring sun was warm. The wall encircled a bit of shrubbery; I could smell the sea-fragrance of broom in flower somewhere. Like a child, Olivier had no hanky and I had to give him mine. He blew his nose and apologized wretchedly.

'I can't believe it,' he said, staring down at the crumpled Kleenex. 'I thought she loved me. I had no idea. I trusted her. And all the time she was seeing those – those men. And Daniel isn't even my son after all.'

'I'm really sorry,' I said. 'I wish there was something I could do to help.'

'I don't know what to do,' he said. 'I've thrown it all away. I didn't want Marie-Paule to file the adultery charge against you. I knew what Luc would do. But she said it was better to have everything out in the open and then we could both be free. I left my wife. We're separated. I can't go home. I don't even dare face my children. Sabine will divorce me and I'll lose everything.'

He started to sniffle again. That was the answer, then, to a problem that had been bothering me. Why had Marie-Paule decided to file for adultery instead of divorcing discreetly by mutual consent, knowing as she must have that Luc would simply riposte in kind? The police, in typical Belgian fashion, had put it down to money. But suppose Olivier had been shilly-shallying about leaving his family and this was her way of forcing his hand? And suppose he hadn't been happy about it? Unhappy enough to kill her?

I could hardly ask him outright. Instead, I said, 'If I were you, I'd go home, tell your wife everything, apologize and promise it'll never happen again. And keep your promise. That's if you want to keep your family together.'

'Do you think she'd forgive me?' he asked, suddenly hopeful.

'She might,' I said. I wouldn't have, personally, but some women will put up with anything to keep home and hearth safe.

'Do you really think that's what I should do?' he asked, staring at me anxiously. I wondered how he managed to get through a day in the office; probably his secretary made all the decisions for him. 'Yes,' I said firmly.

His face cleared up. 'Thank you very much,' he said. 'You're very kind. I'll go now.'

He took my hand and shook it vigorously, then strode off, purpose once more in his stride. I sent up a brief prayer that his wife wouldn't be waiting for him with a hatchet, and went back into the supermarket to find and finish my shopping. I hoped nobody'd nicked my trolley. I remembered a joke Luc had told me about a Swiss guy setting off to do his military service, who left his rifle on the station platform while he ran back home to fetch something he'd forgotten. When he came back, not only was the gun still there, but someone had polished it. This wasn't Switzerland and nobody'd polished my trolley, but my shopping was still there. The fallen melon, however, had been removed.

I do my shopping on foot, since the supermarket's only a stone's throw away from the flat, and I was halfway home when the feeling of being watched returned. This was ridiculous. I stopped and looked round. Nobody suspicious in the street. I pressed on. A voice hissed, 'Madame!'

It was Consuela. She was waiting inside the bus-shelter outside my flat, her face half-hidden by a headscarf, coat collar turned up. She gestured urgently to me to join her, looking round nervously. This was real John Le Carré stuff. I sighed.

'I had to speak to you,' she said desperately. 'It's to tell you that I'm going back to Spain. Tonight.'

'But you can't!' I exclaimed. 'Surely you've been told not to leave the country?'

Her eyes darted from side to side. She seemed on the verge of hysteria.

'Yes, but I'm afraid,' she said in a hoarse whisper, though there was no one around save a few students absorbed in their own business. 'I went back to the police, as you said I should, and I spoke to Monsieur Roland. He was the one I talked to before – a pleasant, kind man. He asked me to describe the men who came to the house. So I did that, and then another policeman came in – a young man with dark hair.'

'Inspector Lebrun,' I said. She nodded.

'He saw me,' she said. 'And then I was afraid and I couldn't say any more.'

'But why not?' I exclaimed.

'Because he was one of them,' Consuela said simply. 'He came twice while I was in the house. I surprised them in the salon, kissing. He was one of her lovers.'

She was pale with fear. I was probably pale with shock.

'And you didn't dare tell Roland?' I asked, grimly. She shook her head. Of course not.

'I was frightened,' she went on. 'And then two days ago this young man came to the house and made threats. If I say anything to the police, he'll have us arrested, my sister and me. So tonight we're both going back to Barcelona. But my sister said I should tell you first.'

'You mustn't go,' I said. 'You must tell Roland the truth. He'll protect you.'

She shook her head, doggedly, stubbornly.

'No. No, we're going home. We're frightened. They're all policemen and we're just foreigners. You can tell them, Madame, in my place. Tell them.'

She pulled her headscarf over her face and set off determinedly down the street, walking so fast she was almost running. There was no point trying to follow her, not with laden shopping bags. Her mind was made up. I could still hardly believe what she'd said. Dear Heaven, how many others were we going to flush out of the wood-work before this was done?

My first inclination was to ring Roland up straight away and spill the beans, but I decided to sleep on it. I was deep in moderately blameless slumber with Hortense wheezing beside me, when the doorbell rang. At first I thought it was the alarm clock, and groped desperately for the bedside table, thinking confusedly that surely I didn't have to go to work today. The doorbell continued to shrill madly. It was five in the morning. I struggled into my dressing gown and staggered out. At the same time, someone rapped loudly and a voice said, 'Police! Open the door!' The whole blessed apartment block must be awake by now. I finally got the door open and uniformed people poured into the apartment, pushing past me and disappearing into the other rooms. Last to come in, looking his usual collected and stylish self, was Inspector Lebrun, negligently waving a piece of official-looking paper, which I suppose was his *mandat de perquisition*. I began to feel aggressive.

'What's going on?' I said, tersely.

He looked me up and down, taking his time. One feels very vulnerable in one's night-clothes.

'We're looking for Luc Vanderauwera,' he said.

'Well, this is the last place he'd be,' I replied, rather sourly.

The troops were reappearing, shaking their heads, lips pursed.

'When did you last see him?' the young man asked. His manner was exceedingly curt.

'Day before yesterday.'

'Where?'

'Antwerp.'

'Do you know where he is?'

'No. Why?' I said, my curtness matching his own.

'Because there's a warrant out for his arrest,' Lebrun said, with just a suspicion of a gloat in his voice. 'For murdering his wife.'

Chapter Thirteen

At seven o'clock on a Sunday morning, the last place I want to be is the police station. Or at any other time, for that matter.

Lebrun really thought he had me where he wanted me. It showed all over the smug face with its pale skin and gold-rimmed glasses. He wasn't bad-looking, if you like the type. I prefer my men on the rugged side. I was feeling less than my usual polished self. They'd given me scarcely enough time to get my clothes on, let alone do anything to my face. Ten years ago it wouldn't have mattered, but these days I need a bit of help at this time in the morning.

'When did you last see Luc Vanderauwera?' was the question which had got the most usage over the last half hour; it was beginning to sound like a music-hall joke. For the umpteenth time, I told him where I'd last seen Luc. Outside Antwerp railway station on Thursday morning. I had gone on a shopping trip and met him by chance. No, I hadn't bought anything.

'You're in a lot of trouble, you know,' Lebrun said, leaning both hands on the desk and staring me in the face. His suit was expensive. Money in the family. Or maybe Marie-Paule had bought them for him? Suppose I asked him?

'Not as far as I know,' I said, staring straight back. 'Is window-shopping a crime these days?'

'We can make life very unpleasant if you don't cooperate,' he said softly.

With difficulty, I stifled a sigh. 'Listen, young man,' I said, 'you're wasting your time. I've been hassled by experts.'

I had, too. I wasn't going to give him the details, though.

I thought I heard a snigger behind me, where a young uniformed poiceman was standing at the door. Lebrun wasn't as sure of himself as he liked to make out. Straightening, his colour higher, he turned away and pulled his cuffs down a little. He was sweating a bit. It couldn't have been the heating in the office, because there wasn't much. There was one old, thickly painted radiator ticking and gurgling under the window.

I pressed my advantage.

'What's more, you haven't any proof that Luc did anything. No weapon, no witnesses, no fingerprints, no evidence. Whoever had this warrant issued needs their head examined.'

'It was Monsieur Gheyssens,' Lebrun said.

Marie-Paule's father. That explained it.

Lebrun went on, 'Vanderauwera's the only one with a real motive. Money.'

'He killed her to prevent her getting his unemployment benefit?' I asked, somewhat ironically.

Lebrun smiled, and I didn't like the smile at all.

'You're not as smart as you think,' he said softly. 'About six months ago, Madame Vanderauwera inherited a large sum of money from an aunt. A very large sum of money. And we all know how hard-up Vanderauwera is, don't we?'

So that's how she was able to buy the house. I wondered if Luc had known. He must have, with that gabby family. All of Lier must have known. I suddenly made my mind up.

'I want to make a statement,' I said. 'I'll talk to Commissaire Roland. No one else.'

'He's not here today,' Lebrun said, staring.

'Then you'd better get him, hadn't you?' I said. 'I'll wait. I've got nothing else to do.'

That wasn't entirely true, but in the event I didn't have to wait long. I managed to coax a cup of coffee and a biscuit out of the young man at the door, who didn't seem to like Lebrun much, and was just finishing up the crumbs when the door opened and Roland came in. From his clothes, I guessed that he'd been about to do a couple of hours' work in the garden. He was, however, his usual urbane self.

'We meet once more, Mademoiselle Haycastle. What's this my young man's been telling me? You wish to make a statement?'

'Yes,' I said. 'I wish to state the following. I've received information to the effect that the Boy Wonder there knew Marie-Paule Vanderauwera rather better than he's been letting on. Very much better. What's more, he's threatened a witness and scared her so much that she's done a runner. Why don't you ask him where *he* was the afternoon Marie-Paule was killed?'

It was hard to beat for dramatic effect. Roland's joviality dropped from him instantaneously; the nondescript twinkling eyes became expressionless as sea-water. 'Who told you?' he asked me. His voice was quiet enough, but I recognize danger when I see it.

'Consuela Garcia,' I replied. 'She came to me yesterday to tell me she and her sister were going back to Spain, because they were too frightened to stay.'

Roland hardly moved. He just turned his head to Lebrun and said, 'Well?'

The young man gaped, his face suddenly putty-coloured. I'd had a small niggling worry that he'd have enough brass to face it out, but he wasn't quite up to it. He struggled for words for a long moment, and the best he could come up with was, 'I didn't kill her. I swear I didn't. You've got to believe me.'

I suppose it's difficult to be original under those circumstances.

98

He gave them a statement without too much persuasion. He and Marie-Paule had been lovers only briefly. Their families knew one another and he'd met her often at police functions in the past. She had terminated the affair after a couple of weeks.

'He has an alibi for that Sunday,' Roland told me some time later. His urbane manner was back, but I was no longer deceived. 'We're running the usual forensic tests, just to make sure. And testing his gun, of course.'

'A Browning?' I asked.

Roland nodded. I remembered Luc once telling me that half the gendarmerie had them.

It was my turn to look at Roland stonily.

'I thought you said that Consuela's evidence was going to be kept confidential?' I said. 'Or does that include telling Marie-Paule's parents and Olivier Delfosse and half of Brussels? No wonder the poor woman ran away.'

'I didn't tell them,' he said abruptly. 'I don't know who did.'

'Lebrun?'

'Maybe. He says not. In any case, that's an internal affair. I'll take care of it.'

Roland was looking at me rather intently, as if trying to make up his mind about something. I hoped he wasn't going to ask me about Luc. I doubted my capacity to lie convincingly under pressure. Or at all, for that matter. Instead, he leaned forward. 'Between you and me, I don't think Vanderauwera did it,' he said abruptly. 'He's far too clever; if he had killed her, he'd have made sure he had a cast-iron alibi. But the warrant was issued over my head. Gheyssens has taken fright at the amount of dirt being dug up on his daughter, and he still has a lot of pull in the force.'

The good ol' boys network again. I refrained from comment.

Roland leaned back in his chair. 'It seems fairly clear that Vanderauwera's been up to something, but that's neither here nor there as far as this enquiry goes. In any case, the murder investigation is far from closed.'

He paused to allow me to speak. I kept my mouth shut.

'Come on,' he said. 'You've been ferreting around. Who do you think did it? The maid, perhaps? She told you she was going back to Spain? We've checked all the flights last night – there weren't any Garcias on the passenger lists.'

'People like Consuela don't fly,' I said. 'They take the train.'

He paused for a fraction of a second. I had the fleeting impression that maybe they hadn't thought of that.

'Well, we'll make enquiries,' Roland continued. 'You said Marie-Paule threatened to have her arrested if she talked? Maybe she got frightened enough to kill?'

'I can't believe it,' I said, frowning. 'She's a devout Catholic. And she needs the job too much. And I saw her when we found the body; she was genuinely distraught. And she's got an alibi.'

'Her sister,' Roland said with a grimace. 'And then there's Olivier Delfosse. No alibi, but no apparent motive. But an emotional man.'

'Yes,' I said slowly, remembering the scene in the supermarket. 'He played me a whole scene about how much he loved her and how shattered he was to find out about the goings-on. But suppose he'd found out about them before? He could have got mad enough to kill her.'

'Suppose indeed,' Roland said.

'He also said that he hadn't wanted Marie-Paule to go for the adultery charge because he knew Luc would name him in return. Maybe he resented her having done it. Suppose he killed her to avoid the publicity? Or because he'd changed his mind about leaving his wife?'

'A little late,' Roland said drily.

'And then there's Sabine Delfosse,' I pursued. 'She had every reason to hate Marie-Paule. Not only had her

100

husband been committing adultery for years, but now they were all going to be dragged through the divorce courts and she was about to lose husband and home, not to mention being humiliated publicly. That's motive enough for murder.'

'She has an alibi,' Roland reminded me.

'Maybe she hired someone to do it?' I suggested.

'Possibly. But this just doesn't have a professional feel about it. There was no breaking-and-entering. Someone just rang the doorbell and walked in that Sunday around two o'clock and shot her. It was sheer luck that they weren't seen. Also, a hired killer would almost certainly have used a silencer and our killer didn't. I don't think we need to look that far away; the answer's nearer home.'

'The mystery lover?'

He shrugged. 'Possibly. Even if he didn't do it, he might have seen something or someone. And there are two other people involved. Doctor Charpentier, and you.'

I stared at him, amazed. 'What possible motive could Marius have?'

'Professional pride – Madame Vanderauwera belittled his medical competence in front of witnesses.'

'He has an alibi,' I protested.

'Yes, he does. And that leaves you. And I have to say, Mademoiselle, that if your alibi wasn't as solid as granite, the warrant would probably have been issued in your name.'

'And what's my motive?' I asked, trying to sound light.

'Jealousy. Frustration over the divorce.'

'Luc and I have split up,' I said. 'And we were already splitting before she was killed. And anyway, I've got that alibi.'

'So you have,' he agreed. 'Fortunately. But perhaps you should consider limiting your involvement in this case now. You're walking on eggshells.'

101

'I promised Daniel I'd find his father,' I said. 'I gave him my word.'

Roland sighed. 'And you're a woman of your word, aren't you?'

And I am, I suppose, uncomfortable though it sometimes is.

The minute I got home, knackered, I had Maggie on the phone.

'Matilda, what on earth's going on? I've had the house crawling with policemen all day – they woke me up at six in the morning and just charged in here like the Light Brigade and they're still here waiting for Luc to come back. Just wait till I see the Chief Inspector – he plays bridge at our club and I'm really going to give him a piece of my mind. *Where's Luc?*'

'I don't know. I've had them here too. They've issued a warrant for Luc and he's gone to ground, I don't know where.'

'But they can't really believe he did it.' Maggie's voice sounded agonized.

'It was Gheyssens who had the warrant issued. Roland doesn't think Luc's guilty.'

'Then why doesn't he tell Gheyssens that?'

'He probably did. Honestly Maggie, I don't think there's any direct evidence against Luc – it's all circumstantial. Roland told me he was carrying on with the investigation.'

'Matilda, we've got to find out who did do it. Can't you please do something? Please?'

'I'm trying,' I said. 'Daniel's away for ten days, so I can drop that enquiry and concentrate on this. But I'm not promising anything.'

'Oh, thank goodness,' Maggie said, her voice full of relief in spite of my last sentence. 'You don't know how grateful I am. I'm feeling so worried. And come and see me again soon. You made a real hit down here. I had both Katrien and Brigitte on the phone for hours banging on about how they admire you, and even Piet rang up and praised you to the skies. By the way, he says the next time you come down, he'll show you his collection. That's a great honour, you've no idea.'

'What does he collect?' I asked with a grimace. 'Milk bottle tops? Seaside postcards?'

'Oh, no,' Maggie said, surprised. 'Nothing like that. Piet collects weapons. Guns, mostly.'

As I put the phone down, my eyes slightly glazed, the doorbell rang. It was Marius. He obviously believed in personal communication.

'I tried phoning but you weren't in. I've got that list for you,' he said, waving an envelope at me.

'What list?' I asked, dazed.

'Addresses and contact names for the various drug-shelters.' He stopped and peered at me closely. 'What's up?' he asked. 'You look bushed.'

I explained about the police raid and the subsequent events.

'May I make a suggestion?' Marius said.

I couldn't think of a way to stop him.

'Get some sleep before you rush off to scour the Brussels drug-scene,' he said. 'About forty-eight hours' sleep. And stay in touch.'

'Will do,' I said.

I even had the hot milky drink this time. So did Hortense and we both slept like tops.

Chapter Fourteen

'My very dear young woman, do you know how many heroin addicts there are in Belgium?'

I didn't, but even if I had, nothing was going to stop this guy from telling me. He was an eminent member of the medical profession and only Marius' name had got me in to see him.

'Thousands,' he said triumphantly. 'Maybe even ten thousand. Not just in Brussels, but all over the country, in all the little towns and villages. Not to mention those who are addicted to cocaine, crack, ecstasy and ordinary medicaments. And you want me to help you find just one. You have no name, no description, no details. I really cannot understand why you are wasting my time.'

He was tall, upright, grey-haired, pince nez'd. He had a goatee beard, which is a thing I loathe, but I didn't like him for a host of other reasons as well. His insufferably arrogant manner, for one. His way of addressing me as if I were indescribably dim-witted, for another. Possibly also the fact that I'd been waiting to see him for hours while a procession of well-dressed women tripped through his waiting room ahead of me. It was late and I was hungry.

The eminent member of the medical profession's *cabinet* was furnished in expensive, heavily luxurious style. He had a vast desk with a dark-green leather top, weighed down by massive silver ornaments, a clutch of imitation Fabergé eggs, a couple of carved malachite ducks and a huge crystal vase with the sort of flower arrangement that you usually find in hotel lobbies. On one side, a dark-green leather sofa and two matching armchairs were grouped cosily round a mahogany and gilt Empire-style coffee table. Half a dozen original pictures hung on the walls. The wall-to-wall carpet was brand new and of considerable plushness. I wondered briefly how much he charged.

'Monsieur le Docteur,' I said, as charmingly as possible under the circumstances, 'Doctor Charpentier told me that you are a leading practitioner in the field of drug addiction.'

'It is one of my many special interests,' he acknowledged, nodding.

'Then you are probably the person best placed to help me. Can't you give me any idea of how I can find this young man? Would he be on one of the government programmes? Do you know of any places in Brussels where I could get information? Cafés or bars or anything like that?'

'Hardly,' he said, smiling superciliously. 'You might try the various drug-prevention centres, but I have to say that they're too busy to be likely to have the time to see you. Now, unless there's anything else—' he half rose, looking at his watch.

I can take a hint as well as the next woman. I got up too and gave him a dazzling smile.

'I really have to thank you, Monsieur le Docteur, for being so very, very helpful,' I said, holding out my hand. 'I really don't know what I'd have done without your assistance.'

It never even occurred to him that I was extracting the Michael. He shook my hand solemnly, accompanied me to the door, and saw me out. His receptionist had gone home already. The street-lights came on just as I stepped out onto the pavement.

The *cabinet* was on the ground floor of a big house in a

105

very posh avenue. You can always tell by the amount of greenery. Rich people have big gardens and lots of trees and bushes. Poor people live in bare streets. This avenue had young cherry trees planted in the pavement, and screens of evergreen and tall shrubs protecting the houses from the road. One or two cars were parked at the kerb. My car was some distance away, as I'd mis-judged the length of the street. I set off down the road. My footsteps echoed – it was really quiet. Up ahead a cat crossed the road, stopping in the middle to have a quick wash. It wasn't cold – maybe we were in for some warmer weather at last.

A sudden sighing of the wind on my left made me turn my head – through a gap in the tall privet hedge I saw a dim open space with the shapes of swings and climbing frames. A children's playground. And then I was grab-bed by the arm and yanked brutally through the hedge; and while I was still reeling off-balance, something hit me hard on the back of the head. It wasn't a stunning blow, but I slipped and staggered and caught the follow-up right on the nose. Any ball-games player can tell you that being hit on the neb is not only excruciatingly pain-ful but also totally incapacitating, at least in the short term. Blinded, eyes watering, face screwed up, I went down under the attack, trying to protect my head with my hands. Then the kicking started. I rolled over and tried to curl up, while my attacker, grunting, almost sob-bing, kicked out again and again. Then, just as abruptly, it stopped. I could hear laboured breathing above me. I opened bleary eyes and squinted sideways in the darkness.

Feet, outlined by the lamps in the street beyond. Tooled leather shoes, polished so the dim light shone on them. Trousers with an elegant turn-up. The hem of a tweedy coat. On the ground beside the feet lay a walking stick with an elaborate handle – in the faint light there was a glint of brassy metal. Then, swiftly, a leather-gloved hand came down and snatched up the stick, and I heard footsteps moving swiftly away through the grass. A tall shadow in a hat and coat passed through the gap in the hedge and the footsteps faded away down the street. A car-door banged. An engine started up.

As the sound faded away, I hauled myself painfully to my knees. I didn't think I was badly hurt, but I thought my nose might be broken. It was bleeding all over my jacket. My face was wet. I groped for a hanky, half sobbing, and mopped tentatively, hardly daring to touch my nose. It was agony. Suppose it healed crooked? I didn't want to go round looking like Gentleman Jim Corbett for the rest of my days.

I felt like lying down again, but I couldn't stay there all night. Staggering, I got myself back to the road. The profound calm of a select residential neighbourhood enveloped me. Nobody about. It was almost a relief. I couldn't have faced the exclamations, the sympathy, or the explanations. I made it to the car and half fell in. My face in the driving mirror was a total mess. There was even grass in my hair. There was dog-dirt on my jacket. That really topped off the evening. Sobbing, I got the key in the ignition and started the car.

I must have been on automatic pilot that night, because I don't really remember making a decision about where to go. But suddenly I found myself in Marius' street. I parked outside his house, got out, rang the doorbell and slumped in a heap on the step, bloody hanky to nose, praying that he was in. If he wasn't, I'd just stay there till he got home.

He was in. I heard steps, the door opened, and I fell backwards into the house.

Marius didn't waste unnecessary time on exclamations. He took care of the first-aid himself, then, ignoring my protests, he put me back in my car, drove me to the clinic, queue-jumped me into the examination room and had me X-rayed. Then they did some very

107

painful things to my nose. It wasn't broken, but the bandage did nothing for my image. They talked about keeping me in. I refused. They compromised. They'd release me into Marius' charge. I agreed, exhausted. Marius drove me back to his house, helped me upstairs to the spare room and put me to bed. I'd long ago given up any interest in the proceedings.

Next morning, I opened my eyes with some difficulty on a pleasant, sunny room with Provençal-style curtains and white pine furniture, and hadn't the faintest idea where I was or what had happened. A cat was curled up at the foot of the bed, just like at home, but this one was small and grey and docile instead of gleaming black and bad-tempered. She looked at me with gentle turquoise eyes and started to purr in anticipation.

My nose hurt. I put a hand up and Marius, from the doorway, said, 'Don't touch.' It must have been the sound of him coming up the stairs which had wakened me.

'It's not broken,' he said. 'But don't mess around with it. How do you feel?'

'Like hell,' I said. 'Shouldn't you be at work?'

'I am,' he answered, rather drily.

'I've got to ring the agency,' I muttered, making an elephantine effort to get out of bed. Marius stopped me.

'I'll fetch a phone,' he said. 'Or if you prefer, I'll do it. But first you'd better tell me what happened.'

I told him, rather thickly.

'Are you going to report it to the police?'

'I don't know yet.'

'Any idea who it was?'

'A man, tall, well dressed, nice shoes, nice gloves. That's all. I didn't see his face, and he didn't say anything.'

'Sure it was a man?'

I stopped to think. I was, though I couldn't say why.

'What did he hit you with?'

'A walking stick, I think. Then he kicked me.'

'Well, he doesn't seem to have been a professional mugger,' Marius remarked. 'You still had your handbag and it doesn't look as if anything's been taken, though you'd better check. And the blows were quite random, as if he were lashing out at you in a temper. You suffered remarkably little damage, apart from bruising. And the nose, of course. A warning, perhaps? In any case, you ought to report it. Would you like some breakfast?'

While he was away, I lay back and pondered. A warning? To get off the case? Not the police, I thought wryly. They were experts; they'd have made a proper job of it. Unless it was Paul Lebrun getting his own back on me for blowing the gaff about him and Marie-Paule. From the height and the type of clothes, it might well have been Olivier Delfosse. It might even have been the eminent member of the medical profession – he'd just about have had enough time to nip out and lie in wait for me if he'd been quick. Had I made that bad an impression?

Marius brought a tray with breakfast and then fetched a telephone, which he plugged into the wall. I did my duty first. My friends at the agency were sympathetic and brisk, asked for a medical certificate, and told me to take things easy till I felt better. Then I had breakfast, with some difficulty because of the nose. The little grey cat came and sat very close, looking intently at the tray, but, unlike Hortense, too polite to snatch. I fed her bits of buttered toast and stroked her ears, and she purred loudly, eyes closed in ecstasy. It's nice to be appreciated. Hortense is parsimonious with her purrs and accepts caresses with an air of royalty receiving her due.

I think Marius must have put a Mickey Finn in my milk, because I started to feel really sleepy after that and could hardly keep my eyes open while my host made speedy arrangements.

'I'll post the medical certificate to your agency and

then I'll drop by your flat and feed your cat,' he said. 'Shall I bring some clothes for you?'

'Marius, you shouldn't put yourself out,' I murmured, already drifting away. 'It's really awfully kind of you. I don't know what I'd have done . . .'

And that was it for the rest of the day.

I was much better the next morning, though I still looked like Jack Nicholson in *Chinatown* and couldn't take deep breaths because of bruised ribs. Marius had to go to work, but he'd made more arrangements.

'My cleaning-lady will be in soon,' he told me briskly. 'She'll get your lunch for you. Stay in bed as much as possible and try not to blow your nose. I'll be back around six.'

My own mother couldn't have looked after me better, but his manner had been exceedingly businesslike, so much so that I hadn't had a chance to thank him as warmly as I'd have liked. He simply hadn't given me an opportunity. He'd put a professional distance between us and I was obliged to respect it. I suppose it was just as well, given the circumstances.

Ten minutes later the doorbell rang and I heard voices in the hall. Footsteps sounded on the stairs and Marius' cleaning lady bounced in, brimming with curiosity. Her name was Yasmina. She was about seventeen, with long pitch-black hair elaborately piled up, and the profile of an Arabian princess. She was wearing loads of make-up and silver jewellery, grungy old black tights, black leotard and sweater. Scheherazade dressed by Oxfam. She was frankly curious about me. Monsieur le Docteur, she said, had never had a lady staying in the house before. Did I know Monsieur le Docteur well? I explained the situation, somewhat laboriously, and Yasmina, perched on the end of the bed, listened with interest, exclaimed suitably, and then, by way of exchange, told me her life-story so far. Her strict father had thrown her out of the house at fifteen because she had refused an arranged marriage, and Marius had helped her and found her work and now she was training to be a social worker and cleaning houses to make money.

She was a whirlwind of activity. She cleaned the house from top to bottom in a morning; I could track her progress through the building by the sound of Arab pop-music from her transistor radio. Then she cooked lunch and we ate together, the cat sitting to attention, delicately taking titbits from Yasmina's thin, quick hands with their silver bangles. The cat's name was Minette, which is French for Tiddles. Yasmina, looking at me slyly sideways under long black lashes, pursued the subject of Marius, which was obviously on her mind. She thought he liked me. A lot. I liked him too, I said, but I had just broken up with my boyfriend and was temporarily off the market. A pity, said Yasmina. She was a romantic. Well, we all are at seventeen.

Yasmina left at three o'clock and the house seemed very quiet without her. I got up and wandered into the bathroom to examine my battered dial. I wouldn't be winning any beauty contests for a day or two. I had a shower, feeling very thoughtful. It sounded as if Marius were smitten, which explained the carefully professional manner. I did like him a lot, but it's never 'off with the old, on with the new' with me. I wanted to be on my own for a while. A pity. A waste.

I was no nearer a decision about telling the police what had happened. I thought I ought to, but frankly dreaded it. More hours in the police station. More suspicion. More hassle.

The house was spotless. I put the kettle on for tea and stood looking out of the kitchen window. It was invitingly sunny out; a few clumps of bright tulips stood about, and the new leaves on the lilac were green and tender. April already. Cup of tea in hand, I wandered into the living-room and browsed along the bookshelves. Marius was an eclectic and multilingual reader. An intelligent, cultured man. Just my type. The house was silent around me, but friendly. I felt at home there. I sat down at the table to read, pushing aside some papers that Yasmina must have forgotten to tidy away. Then I recognized them. Daniel's drawings of Marius and me.

I picked them up, smiling, and then stopped smiling. I'd barely glanced at the other drawings in the sheaf when Marius had first shown them to me, but now I stared in disbelief. One was clearly of a nurse in the hospital, big and jolly and rather buck-toothed. The fourth was Consuela, and the fifth a sharp-faced young man with long hair and a cigarette drooping out of the corner of his mouth, very much like the comic strip cowboy Lucky Luke. It was remarkable how truly Daniel's eye had caught the essence of his subjects, though surely a child of ten could hardly have analysed this consciously: Consuela's heavy glumness, Marius' square honesty, the nurse's jolly boisterousness. The young man looked unmistakably like a good-for-nothing.

So who was he? Marie-Paule's unknown lover?

I'd put money on it, myself.

Marius, when he got back that evening, agreed that it might be, though cautiously. 'When does Daniel get back from the mountains?'

'Tuesday,' I said. 'Five days to wait. By the way, I've decided to go to the police.'

'Good,' Marius said approvingly. 'I didn't want to push you, but I think it's best.'

He was busy with pots and pans. I looked at his back and said, as casually as I could, 'You've looked after me really well, but I think I'd better go home tomorrow. I've imposed on you quite long enough.'

There was a very brief pause, then he said, quite normally, 'You can stay as long as you like, you know. It's no trouble.'

'I really ought to get back. Hortense must be missing me.'

'Whatever you decide,' Marius said, turning round. 'Would you mind passing over that courgette, please?'

So, no torrid declarations. His restraint was positively English. Maybe Yasmina was wrong after all. But my nose, battered as it was, told me differently.

Chapter Fifteen

I rang the police the next day and went straight round to make a statement. It wasn't as bad as I'd expected. Perhaps my purple nose made them sympathetic. Roland wasn't around, for which I was grateful. Then I went home. Hortense sniffed suspiciously at my clothes, as if sensing that I'd been talking to strange cats, but was unexpectedly pleased to see me and settled down on my lap for a snooze. I snoozed too. I wasn't feeling very energetic; Marius had warned me about that. Shock to the system, he'd said. Don't fight it. So I didn't. I was off work till the end of the week.

I had a quiet weekend. A bit of housework, a lot of television. Nobody called, for a change. The weather was sunny – everybody in the apartment-block seemed to be springcleaning. Housewives in cotton overalls hung perilously from second-floor casements with window-cleaning implements in their hands, while Hoovers hummed like bees all round. I filled my window-boxes with earth and planted seeds, wishing for the first time that I had a proper garden, like Marius, instead of a mere balcony. Hortense tight-roped along the balustrade edge, tail raised, nonchalant. It was a relief to be on our own. I cooked myself a nice supper on Saturday night and had half a bottle of good wine with it. On Sunday I went for a walk in the park. The warm weather had held for a few days now and everything was stirring. The solitude did me good.

Marius came round on Sunday evening to check my progress and said I could go back to work, which was rather funny considering I had no work to go back to. He asked if I were going to see Daniel on Tuesday to ask about the picture.

'I'll go round in the evening,' I said. 'It must be someone Daniel's seen several times, and he must surely know the name. Then I'll try the drug-prevention centres. They might be more helpful than your eminent friend.'

'He's no friend of mine,' Marius said frowning. 'He made a few useful discoveries thirty years ago and has lived off them ever since, lending his name to select committees and making a mint from rich ladies' Valium habits.' He stopped for a moment, and I glanced at him, remembering something similar he'd said about himself. However, he resumed, 'But, Matilda, I've been thinking about this, and I reckon it would be helpful if I came along. I know some of those people and they might be more prepared to give up their precious time to a colleague. If you don't mind, that is?'

'I don't mind at all,' I said. 'But can you spare the time? You said you were really busy.'

'I can squeeze you in,' he said. 'Call me when you've spoken to Daniel.'

The trouble was, I didn't get to see Daniel. The maid who answered the door gawped at the sight of my face, and when I asked for Daniel, stammered and stuttered and finally said he wasn't in. Had he come home from the mountains, I asked. She said yes, then no, then went red and glanced round desperately behind her, as if for help. Poor thing, she was a lousy liar. What was all this? I asked if I could speak to Agnès. The maid, giving up all pretence of diplomacy, said she'd been told not to let me in. I stood firmly on the doorstep and asked her please to tell Agnès that I needed to speak to her on a matter of urgency. And from inside the house, Agnès' voice said,

115

'What's the matter, Louise? Who is it?'

I walked past the maid into the hall and said, 'I have to speak to Daniel, Madame Gheyssens. It's very important.'

She was standing at the foot of the stairs, one hand on the balustrade, elegant as usual in a Wedgwood blue suit which looked like Chanel and probably was. She said, 'Thank you, Louise,' and the maid nodded and disappeared thankfully. Agnès came down the stairs towards me and stopped dead, her mouth open.

'But what happened to your face?' she said in horror.

'I was attacked,' I said. 'Never mind that now. I really need to see Daniel. If he can identify this picture, we might be able to find out who killed Marie-Paule.'

I don't think she was listening to me at all. Her horrified eyes were fixed on my bruises, her hand up to her own face.

'When did it happen?' she asked. Her lips were trembling.

'Tuesday night,' I replied, a little surprised at her reaction. 'It's OK, it's getting better now. You should have seen me on Wednesday. Can I see Daniel, please?'

She managed to pull herself together, with an effort.

'I'm sorry,' she said. 'My husband has forbidden me to admit you into the house, let alone see Daniel, and he may come back at any moment. I must beg you to leave.'

'But this is really important,' I protested.

'Then you should tell the police,' she said. 'We don't want Daniel upset any more. You must understand that.'

I paused to consider. I could hardly force my way upstairs. On the other hand, they couldn't keep Daniel shut up for ever.

'OK,' I said. 'I don't want to cause you any trouble. I'll go quietly.'

'I'm sorry,' she said again. This woman seemed to spend her life apologizing.

Outside in the street, I paused again. The kids were on

Easter holiday already, so I couldn't get hold of Daniel at school. I was pinning my hopes on Daisy. Dogs need to be walked, and I was betting that Daniel wouldn't want to be separated from his new love after ten whole days away. He'd have to take her out and I'd be waiting.

Ten out of ten, Matilda.

I was outside the house in my car at eight the next morning, hoping the Gheyssens were early risers. At nine, out came Daniel, with Daisy on a lead, and the elderly Mediterranean lady in attendance. They set off, slowly, because Daniel and Daisy hadn't got the hang of the lead yet and kept getting themselves tied up in knots. There was a small park down the road and I made a bet with myself that that's where they were going. I drove past them, parked the car and waited for them just inside the park gates. Right again. In they came. The old lady sat down on a bench and took some knitting out of a bag, while Daniel let Daisy off the lead. She promptly shot off into a large bank of rhododendrons, barking wildly, with Daniel in hot pursuit. I intercepted them on the other side.

'Mathilde!' he exclaimed, his face shining with pleasure. I got an enthusiastic kiss on the cheek.

'I came to see you last night,' I explained, 'but your grandmother wouldn't let me in.'

'She's worried right now,' Daniel said. 'Because Papie's not feeling very well. I had a super time in the mountains. We didn't have much snow, though.'

He was brown and healthy-looking, his eyes sparkling.

'Have you found my father yet?' he asked, buoyantly.

'Not yet, but I think I'm making progress,' I said. 'I need your help today. Who's this?'

And I held out the drawing of the young man with the cigarette. There was no hesitation.

'That's Christian,' Daniel said. 'He was a friend of Maman's. He used to come to the house now and then.'

117

'Do you know his other name?'

Daniel shook his head, then took the drawing from my hand.

'It's not very good, this one,' he said. 'I couldn't get the eyes right.'

'I think it's brilliant,' I said. 'Listen, Daniel, I don't think your Mamie wants me to come to the house any more, but when I have news about your father, I'll be in touch. OK?'

'But what about tea?' Daniel protested. 'And we said we'd go to the BD museum.'

'I'm still on for that, pet,' I said. 'But we can't go unless your grandmother gives her permission. See what she says and give me a call. You know what my number is.'

'All right,' Daniel said. 'I've got this for you.'

It was a snapshot of himself in the snow, grinning under one of those daft Norwegian knitted hats with reindeer prancing round them and a bobble on top.

A voice called his name rather querulously from the other side of the hedge, and Daniel wrapped his arms round me, gave me a hasty hug, and disappeared, followed by Daisy, still yapping. I made my way back to the car, thoughtfully. I now had a name and a picture, but was that going to be enough?

Chapter Sixteen

Marius' desire to help me was well intentioned, but it effectively reduced the amount of time we were able to spend on the search to the evenings, after his work ended. As for me, the agency managed to pick up a few hours' work audio-typing, in a small office where everyone studiously avoided staring at my face. I expect they thought my boyfriend beat me up. For the rest of the week and the beginning of the next, I met Marius at six and we did the rounds of the clinics and drug prevention centres. Having a doctor along certainly helped matters; we met with nothing but cooperation from the busy personnel. In the event, we struck gold on the fourth night. Somebody recognized the picture. Christian Lemaître, aged twenty-five, former heroin addict.

'One of our success stories,' added our informant, somewhat cynically. 'Complete cure. Now he's one of the most successful dealers. Makes you sick, doesn't it? All that money spent and now he's out there hooking more benighted brats with nothing better to do.'

'What's he like?' I asked.

'Clever, cheeky, chats up anything in skirts. *Un vrai dragueur* – had all the nurses eating out of his hand. No moral sense whatever. An interesting psychological case in many ways, because he's no fool.'

'Address?'

He gave an address in Ixelles, my own commune, adding, 'You can always tell when he's at home because there's a red Mazda parked out in the street. Also he hangs out a lot at a local café – Chez Moumou. That's where he does a lot of his dealing. The University's a big customer, and the local secondary schools.'

Marius shifted in his chair and muttered something, and the man behind the desk, a tired, bespectacled person of about my own age, looked at him and nodded.

'I know,' he said, 'all those middle-class kids with no worries and the whole of life at their fingertips. What makes them do it? God knows. I don't. At least the North African kids in Saint-Gilles have some excuse. It makes me wonder why I bother.'

The Belgian medical profession seemed to be suffering from a case of the collective glums.

'My great-aunt used to say that every good deed counts,' I said firmly. 'And I still believe her after nearly thirty-six years. You need a couple of days off, preferably somewhere warm in good company.'

A faint smile appeared behind the specs. 'That's the best advice I've had for years,' he said. 'If I complain to my colleagues, they ask me if my habits are regular and prescribe castor oil.'

I didn't tell him that it was the same great-aunt who used to disinfect dogs.

As I was putting the key in the ignition, Marius said, 'Right. Now for the police station.'

I stopped what I was doing and said, 'What?'

'We've got to tell Roland straight away and have this Christian picked up. Then they can get the whole thing sorted out.'

'Wait a minute here,' I said. 'If the police get hold of him, we'll never find out what his story is. It'll disappear into the files at police headquarters and we'll be as much in the dark as ever. We've got to talk to him first.'

Marius stared as if I were crazy.

'Matilda, you can't. He might be the murderer. It's ridiculous. It's dangerous. You can't do it.'

'Yes, I can,' I said. 'You don't know the police like I do.

If Gheyssens really wants to get Luc for this, he's quite capable of suppressing evidence, particularly if it's prejudicial to his daughter. And this is bound to be.'

'Roland wouldn't let him,' Marius protested.

'Roland wouldn't be given the choice.'

Marius, a man of limited patience, stopped arguing and issued an ultimatum.

'If you don't go to the police, I will,' he announced.

There was a short silence.

'You'll blow the case,' I said.

'I don't care.'

'At least give me twenty-four hours.'

'To let yourself get beaten up again, or worse? Nothing doing. This is a police job. Well, are we going, or aren't we?'

'You may be,' I said, 'but I'm not,' and I took the key out of the ignition and sat back.

Marius got out of the car without a word and started marching off down the street. Blast and damn, on a number of counts. I wondered if he'd call the police or go in person. Either way, I'd have to move fast.

I got to Chez Moumou just before eleven. It was crowded and smoky, a typical Belgian working-class café with a big brightly lit bar and wooden chairs and tables. At the back were a few dim booths with wood partitions. A large hairy dog lay just inside the door, nose down, fast asleep. You had to step over him to get inside.

My bruises looked just right in this kind of place. To add verisimilitude, I'd messed my hair up, slapped on some careless make-up and opened my blouse one button lower. It seemed to work – I heard a few dubious compliments as I pushed my way to the bar. I ordered a brandy, and when it came, I asked the barman casually if Christian was around. He looked me up and down with an air of genial contempt and said, what, another one? Always some tart chasing that Christian. Urgent, was it? Yes, I said. It always was, said the barman.

Two hours went by. A bar stool became vacant; I

bagged it gratefully. My feet were killing me. I got my powder compact out, leaned on the bar, and started applying lipstick ostentatiously. Nothing like that to make one look like a slag. In the mirror, I cautiously surveyed the room behind me. Nobody seemed to be looking at me more than was normal.

A soft voice in my ear said, '*Tu me cherches, ma belle?*' and I jumped. The lipstick fell on the bar.

He was about my height, slim, with the sort of impudent boyish air that some women find irresistible. I'm not one of them, but I could see the attraction. A thin face, a slightly vicious mouth, knowing grey eyes, longish rumpled hair. He wore jeans, running-shoes, and a leather jacket very much like Luc's, over a white T-shirt with the name of some American university on the front. He looked me up and down very thoroughly and the smile intensified.

'Can we talk?' I said. 'Somewhere quiet?'

He was used to this. He led me to a booth in the furthest corner of the café, had a word with the two men in it, who decamped with sidelong glances at me, and invited me to sit down. Across the table, he leaned back with narrowed eyes and said lazily, 'How did you get my name?'

'From Marie-Paule,' I said. 'She recommended you.'

He smiled like a little boy, unworriedly.

'Oh, I see,' he said. Then he added, 'She's probably told you I'm expensive. But then, she can afford it. I might consider a discount for you.'

I wondered if my astonishment showed on my face. Either he was the world's next Laurence Olivier or else he didn't know she was dead. But I was no Vivien Leigh. I couldn't react quickly enough. As I fumbled for words, his face lost all semblance of good humour and his hand shot out and gripped my wrist, so hard it hurt.

'What the hell's all this about?' he said.

I took a chance. Gritting my teeth, I stared into the

slitted grey eyes and said, 'She's dead. Marie-Paule's dead. She was murdered just after your last visit to her, a month ago.'

He let go of my wrist and sat back, his face quite blank with shock. '*Merde*,' he said. Automatically he fumbled for a cigarette, lit it, and took a drag. '*Merde*,' he said again, and again, '*Merde*.' Then he looked up at me, his face full of suspicion. 'Are you the police?'

'No,' I said, rubbing my wrist. 'But I think they'll be onto you pretty soon. You didn't know she was dead?'

He shook his head. 'She calls me when she wants me to come over. She hadn't called, that's all. How was she killed?'

'Shot,' I said. 'They know she had a lover there that day and soon they're going to know it was you. I wanted to talk to you first.'

'Why?'

'Because they think her husband did it and he's a friend of mine,' I said.

'The ex-cop? Well, maybe he did. He's a tough bastard and they hated one another.'

'I know he didn't kill her,' I said.

'Well, neither did I,' Christian said, taking another drag at the cigarette. 'For Christ's sake, why should I? She was my best customer.'

'What time did you leave her house that day?'

'Just after one. Maybe a quarter past.'

'Did you see anybody around when you left? In the street, I mean? Or did anyone come to the house?'

'Nobody came. And I didn't see anyone. No, wait a minute. I saw the maid. You know, that Spanish maid of Marie-Paule's. She was walking down the road towards the house as I was leaving.'

'The maid!' I said, in astonishment. 'Are you sure?'

'It was her all right. Middle-aged woman in a dark-blue coat, scarf, hat, dark hair.' He was beginning to get twitchy. He finished the cigarette, stubbed it out, and got up.

123

'Walk out with me,' he ordered.

I didn't get any choice. He took my arm in a painful grip and hustled me out through the crowd into the darkness. It was quiet outside. He dropped my arm and turned to look at me. 'I'm getting out of here,' he said. The bravado was coming back. 'Pity we couldn't do business,' he said. Light from the café glinted on his sharp teeth. Then he was off, walking quickly down the street.

I got out of there too, quickly, but outside my apartment block, I sat in the car for a while, thinking. Had Consuela lied, after all? I remembered the sight of her when she opened the door to Marius and me. Dark-blue coat and scarf, all right. Woollen hat and dark hair. It couldn't all have been an act, surely? Or could it? I wasn't sure any more. A movement caught my eye: my upstairs neighbour, Monsieur Penne, walking his fat little dog, Titus. I got out of the car slowly, realizing how tired I was. Monsieur Penne likes to talk, even at dead of night. I listened to his tale of insomnia and bad dreams with half a brain, while Titus snuffed round my feet. We all went in together. Monsieur Penne looked rather startled when he saw me in the light, but said nothing. My last thought before I fell asleep was of Marius.

I thought of Marius again when the doorbell rang the next afternoon. It was half-past three; I'd just got back after an unproductive six hours in the office. But in the event, it wasn't Marius, it was Commissaire Roland. He was alone. He walked into my flat without a word and stood looking at me. He looked tired.

'Well,' I said, 'did Christian Lemaître talk?'

To my surprise, there was no answer. Instead, Roland took his hat off, dropped it on a table, sat heavily down on the sofa and said, 'As a matter of fact, no. He couldn't. He's dead.'

Chapter Seventeen

My legs turned to sticks of Emmenthal cheese and began to wobble. I sat too.

'When?' I said, my voice a bare squeak.

'In the early hours of the morning. Doctor Charpentier made a statement last night, but it wasn't passed on to me till this morning at eight. When we got to Lemaître's apartment, we found him dead. There had been a struggle and he'd been battered to death. We found drugs hidden in the flat. All the signs indicate it was a settling of accounts – maybe a rival dealer or a dissatisfied customer. He seems to have been a nasty piece of work with plenty of enemies. Neighbours heard voices around three o'clock: men's voices. Said there was a scuffle. Nobody interfered, of course. You saw Christian Lemaître last night?'

I was in no state to deny it. I'd suddenly realized that I was playing a very dangerous game.

'What time?' Roland pursued.

'Around one o'clock in the morning. In the café, Chez Moumou. We talked for about fifteen minutes, then left.'

He looked at me silently for a moment. 'So you last saw him around a quarter past one? What did you do then?'

'I came straight home.'

'Did anyone see you?'

'My upstairs neighbour, Monsieur Penne.'

There was another silence. Then he said, 'That's very

125

fortunate for you. Otherwise I'd have to arrest you as a possible suspect.'

I went hot and cold. 'What possible motive could I have for killing Christian?' I exclaimed.

'To suppress information implicating your friend Mr Vanderauwera,' Roland said quietly.

'He didn't have any,' I said. 'I'll swear he didn't even know Marie-Paule was dead. He hadn't heard from her since that Sunday – it was usually she who called him. He admitted he'd been there, but he said he left just after one. The only thing he told me is that he saw Consuela coming back to the house as he was leaving.'

'The maid?' Roland said, frowning. 'Was he sure?'

'Positive.'

He sat for a moment thinking. 'I'll have to have her brought back from Spain,' he said. 'The trouble is, no one knows where she is; I've been in touch with the Barcelona police.'

He looked at me for a long moment, and his face showed nothing but weariness.

'Lemaître was packing to leave when the killer found him,' he said. 'You warned him he was about to be denounced?'

My face must have answered him.

'Miss Haycastle, last time we met I gave you some well-meant advice,' he said. 'Now I'm telling you. Stay out of this from now on. You've already got yourself knocked about and you don't know how close you've come to getting into serious trouble. I know you mean well, but this isn't a game for amateurs. Leave it to us. I'll see myself out.'

But at the door, he turned again.

'By the way, maybe you haven't heard, but we've arrested Vanderauwera. Up in the Ardennes. He says he's been on a camping holiday and didn't know there was a warrant out for him. If you believe that, you'll believe anything.'

126

'He didn't do it,' I said. My heart was in my boots.

'Maybe not, but it'll keep Gheyssens off my back for the time being. Remember what I said, stay out of trouble.'

I sat for a while after he'd gone, feeling ill. The inside of a prison cell had never loomed so near. And at the bottom of my stomach was a sick feeling. They'd got Luc. He'd have to tell them about the car-stealing scam now, or risk the murder charge. Either way, it wasn't a very bright prospect.

Maybe I was getting too old for this kind of caper. Maybe I should take up tatting instead.

Marius called that night, rather shame-faced, if you can be shame-faced over the phone.

'I know I put you in a difficult position,' he said. 'I wanted to say I'm sorry.'

'That's OK,' I replied. 'John Wayne.'

'I beg your pardon?'

'John Wayne. "A man's gotta do what a man's gotta do." It's just a pity your statement took so long to get to Roland. If they'd passed it on immediately it might have made all the difference.'

'It was the middle of the night,' Marius said. 'I had trouble getting anyone to listen at all. Are you in hot water?'

'Strong hints were dropped that I could be arrested on suspicion of murder, not to mention conspiring to pervert the course of justice. But in the end, Roland just rapped me over the knuckles and told me to mind my own business.'

'Can I hope you'll take his advice?' Marius asked.

'I'm thinking about it. Did you know Luc's been arrested?'

'So I hear. It was only a matter of time. Belgium's a small country. He should have gone abroad.'

'That would have made him look guilty,' I said. 'He knows all the angles.'

'I'm sure he does. By the way, could you face another vegetarian meal soon?'

I had to laugh. 'I expect so. But it's my turn. Why don't you come here and I'll see what I can do. When are you free?'

We fixed a date for the following week and rang off. I was feeling better. At least Marius and I were still friends.

I debated whether or not I should charge off down to Saint-Gilles prison to visit Luc, perhaps with an iron file baked into a cake. I decided that discretion was the better part of valour. If he wanted me to visit, he'd no doubt let me know. He had a clever lawyer. He might even get bail, though I doubted it, knowing Gheyssens' influence. In the meanwhile, we all just had to sit it out. But I couldn't banish the sick feeling at the thought of him sitting in a prison cell, no matter what he'd done.

Daniel called on Friday night, very down-in-the-mouth. 'I can't come to the museum,' he said. 'Papie's still not feeling well and Mamie's worried about him and I couldn't persuade her. I don't know what the matter is. Everybody's acting funny. Papie's going to the coast tomorrow for a rest.'

Belgians have a tremendous and touching faith in the beneficial properties of North Sea air, and make the most of their short stretch of coastline. Frankly, I'd take the Mediterranean any time; sitting on a cold grey beach staring at oil-rigs and cross-Channel ferries isn't my idea of fun. But the Gheyssens probably had an apartment or villa, like most well-heeled subjects of King Albert. I had a bet with myself it would be at Knokke. I supposed that Pierre Gheyssens was allowing himself a little relaxation, now that his son-in-law was safely behind bars. I wondered what they'd told Daniel. Whatever it was, it wouldn't be the truth.

'I expect they'll let us go later,' the little voice said over the phone, as if trying to reassure me. 'We'll just have to be patient. Will you call me if you have any news, Mathilde?'

'Of course I will. Take care of yourself, pet.'

'I've got to go,' he said again hurriedly, and put the phone down.

The call reminded me that I still had promises to keep – I was no nearer finding Daniel's father than I had been at the beginning. The next step was the PR agency where Marie-Paule had worked ten years ago. I wondered rather pessimistically what the chances were that the same people would still be working there – staff turnover in that kind of business is fierce. But I could only try. The agency had a job lined up for me which looked as if it would run for several months. The trouble was, it didn't start for two weeks. Never mind, I'd be able to show my face in the bank again soon. In the meantime, my time was my own. And now it was the weekend again.

It was a long, long time since I'd been to the cinema, so I went and saw the latest Merchant-Ivory, which was top of the viewing lists in Brussels. They love all that turn-of-the-century English upper-crusty stuff here; it confirms all their worst fears about the English class-system. I came out thinking for the trillionth time how much I'd like to be a film producer. I'd forgotten how crowded the Rue Neuve area gets on a Saturday. The people were wall-to-wall. My car was parked miles away. Half way there, I realized that the Centre Belge de la Bande Dessinée was only a fraction out of my way, and I altered course. Why not? At least I could tell Daniel what to expect.

I certainly hadn't expected to find Art Nouveau décor, but that was what I got. Not any old Art Nouveau either. It was Victor Horta. The BD centre was in a restored linen and fabric store, a miracle of glass and steel, slender white columns, wrought iron and cool grey light. The huge open foyer was paved with mosaic, a graceful, five-globed lamppost in the middle. There were schoolkids

129

everywhere. I paid my money and walked upstairs, fascinated. The whole ceiling was glass, designed to let the shoppers see the true colours of the fabrics.

The first floor had a display showing how you put a BD together: from the scenario to the drawing, through the colouring and inserting of text to the printing and marketing. The colouring techniques seem to vary widely: some artists use spray, others airbrush, some use computers and others work from photographs. Some BDs are genuine works of art. I wandered through what they call 'The Treasure' – a collection of original BD plates from a range of different artists. This section wasn't crowded; I could hear the schoolkids chattering away like starlings in some other part of the museum, but up here it was quiet.

High up near the glass roof there was a whole section on Hergé and his immortal offspring. BDs are an excuse to indulge in childhood again. I went from picture to picture with a delighted grin on my face: Tintin's eternal boyish eagerness, Captain Haddock in red-faced spluttering rage, Snowy face-to-face with a trio of irritable geese, the Thompsons, who manage to be both inimitably English and inimitably Continental, and a whole wall of Hergé animals ranging from snooty llamas to scowling vultures. It was wonderful.

In another room, an exhibition explored Hergé's *belgitude* (pretentious word) through another of his creations, the Etterbeek urchins Quick and Flupke. It's a world where Belgian housewives in flowery pinnies stand frowning on doorsteps with brooms in their hands, and little kids absorbed in comics bring the Gare du Midi tram screeching to a halt in the street. The organizers had even simulated a rainy Brussels day with dripping water and the faint, familiar clang of a tram bell.

The people were beginning to come in as I moved up to the third floor. The museum is relatively new and there was a lot of unused space up there, but they had a special exhibition of young, up-and-coming BD artists. A bunch of fifteen-year-old girls were giggling over one exhibit; I pushed past them and stopped in front of a plate whose fresh, spring-like colours reminded me of something. And then I stood still, staring, while the teenagers jostled past.

I'm no art expert, but I didn't have to be. The techniques, the use of colour, the whole spirit of the drawing was instantly recognizable. I hardly needed to see the small 'J' in the bottom corner to know that this had to be he same artist who'd done Marie-Paule's portrait. My heart bounded; here was the most unexpected piece of good luck. This man had known Marie-Paule ten years ago – if anybody could give me the information I needed about her, he could. So who was he? My eyes searched for and fell on the label. It said simply 'Jerzy' and underneath that, '1960–1982'.

Oh God, he was dead, then.

Chapter Eighteen

'Run over by a train,' said the assistant curator in the office downstairs, adjusting her spectacles and peering through them at the card in her hand. 'Ten years ago. I remember. Terribly sad. So much talent. Of course, we all suspected it was suicide, but they were Catholics, so it went down as an accident, foggy night, and all that. Poles, you know.'

I missed that. 'Pardon me?' I said.

'He was Polish. Jerzy Raczkowski. Wonderful technique. He did it all himself, the drawing and colouring. Gouache. But he couldn't get a good story so he never made a breakthrough.'

'You knew him?' I asked.

'Only a little. Strange boy.'

'How?'

'Well, you get all sorts in this business,' she said. 'Most of the artists are practical people earning a living, but you get the odd one who's working out his own private fantasies and ends up not being able to tell fantasy from reality. You create a dream-world and then you get sucked into it and become so absorbed that you can't keep your feet on the ground. He was a bit like that. A dreamer. Not quite in touch.'

'A friend of mine has a portrait by him,' I said. 'Done about ten years ago, I suppose. I wanted to talk to him about it.'

'Well, his mother's still living in Brussels,' the assistant curator said, looking at me sympathetically. 'You could try there. We've got the address.'

I bought Daniel a jigsaw puzzle crowded with cartoon characters, and went out thoughtfully. What a temptation, to create your own beautiful world and escape into it. I suppose artists of all sorts do it all the time. Reality's a daunting prospect and there aren't many choices: confront it, escape from it, or go down under it. I've always taken the first choice, but I can understand the temptation of the second.

I thought long and hard about going to see Jerzy Raczkowski's mother. After all, you can't just waltz in and start asking people questions about their son who committed suicide. I wished I had some credentials, that I could say with truth that I was a real investigator and not just a Nosy Parker on the side. It was really only the thought of Daniel that got me there on Sunday morning.

It was a small terraced house in an unfashionable part of town. The tiny front gardens reflected the different personalities of the house-owners: gay spring bulbs here, and rank grass and groundsel there. The garden I was standing in had clumps of crocuses and primulae, a neat gravel path all of two metres long, and the long stems and starry flowers of clematis montana round the front door. There was no answer to the doorbell. I craned back to look up at the house. It needed painting, but there were neatly looped lace curtains at the windows and flowering plants on the window-sills.

Clearly, nobody was in. I backed out and closed the gate. Then I remembered what day it was, recalling the sound of church bells on the edges of consciousness. She was a Catholic. She'd be at Mass. I got back in the car and waited. A couple of children crouched on the pavement, playing some incomprehensible game. An elderly couple went by on their way to lunch with relatives or friends, judging by the little bunch of flowers and the square box of *pâtisseries* in their hands. Then down

133

the street, I saw a woman approaching, short and square and slow. I got out of the car to have a better look. She checked slightly when she saw me, and I suddenly had the idea that this was the woman I wanted to see. I waited. She was in her sixties, with fair hair in unenthusiastic waves and a broad face. Steady grey eyes watched me as she came nearer. When she was about six feet away, she stopped, four-square.

'Madame Raczkowska?' I asked, and she said, 'Yes.'

'I'm trying to find out some information about something that happened ten years ago, and I thought you might be able to help me. It's about somebody who knew your son.'

The face was as steady as ever. It was the kind of face that hid nothing, because it had nothing to hide.

She said, 'My son is dead.'

'I know. But I thought that perhaps you could tell me something. You see, this little boy has just lost his mother, and I promised him I'd try and find out who his father is. Your son painted a picture of his mother ten years ago and I wanted to ask him about her.'

Unaccustomed nervousness had made me unusually incoherent. It had struck me anew just how much of a cheek this was. I was just revising my story when she said, rather puzzled, 'But which little boy?'

I had a brainwave, then. I opened my handbag and hauled out the photo Daniel had given me, of himself in the reindeer hat.

'That's him,' I said, holding it out. 'That's Daniel.'

With great deliberation, she opened the clasp of her handbag, took out a spectacle case, opened that too, and put the spectacles on. Then she took the picture from my hand.

She looked at it for a long, long time, and her face hardly changed at all. Then she looked at me and said, 'Come inside.'

It seemed to take her a long time to get the key in

134

the lock. It was a tiny house. I stood awkwardly in the crowded front room. Madame Raczkowska picked a framed photograph up off the sideboard and held it out to me.

She said, 'This is my son, when he was ten years old.'

I looked at the other little boy in the picture, and the stuffing in my legs went.

'But this is Daniel,' I said. Then, looking again at the background, the clothes, the style, I said, 'No, it can't be.'

'That is my son,' she said again. And this time, she looked at the gay snapshot in her own hand and I saw her swallow.

The faces were absolutely identical.

She showed me a photo taken just before her son's death, and the resemblance was still unmistakable. Some parents and children don't look anything like one another. Most often, there are a few recognizable features. But sometimes by a startling genetic freak the face is repeated in total exactness; we've all seen mothers and kids in the street who are carbon-copies of one another. Daniel, in all innocence, had remarked that Olivier couldn't be his father because he didn't look like him. Without knowing anything about it, he was absolutely right. Now, by the same token, I was looking at the face of a man who couldn't have been anything other than Daniel's father, and no amount of genetic testing would have convinced me otherwise in a million years.

Madame Raczkowska made coffee, and then sat with the picture of Daniel in front of her, while I carefully explained the whole story. It took a little while. She said nothing, but her eyes were on the photograph all the while. From time to time she caressed it with her thick fingers, as if it were Daniel himself. After all, he was her grandchild. When I finished, there was a long silence.

Then she said, 'I knew there was someone. He never talked about her, never brought her here, but I knew there was someone. I could smell her on his clothes when

135

he came home. He was a different person, those last few months. At first he was happy, happier than he'd been since he was a little boy. Then he became unhappy. More and more unhappy. He wouldn't talk to me. It was very difficult. We'd been very close since my husband died and suddenly he stopped talking to me. And then – you know what happened. An accident, they said, but it was no accident. I am a Catholic, but not a fool. It does not matter – I know God will forgive him.' She looked at the photo again and said, with a slight tremble in her voice, 'What is he like, Daniel?'

'He draws very well,' I said. 'He's had a tough time, but he's determined and bright and very talented.'

'Are you going to tell him?' she asked quietly.

'I think he needs to know,' I replied. 'He needs to know he's got another grandmother – someone who can talk to him about his father.'

She nodded. Then unexpectedly, she rose to her feet and said, 'Come.'

I followed her up the narrow stairs to the very top of the house. There was a locked door, which she opened, and I knew immediately where I was.

'This is Jerzy's studio,' she said. 'We had the window put in specially. I have let no one in here since he died. All his work is in that cupboard. You must look, now. I must go downstairs and think.'

As her heavy footsteps receded on the stairs, I looked round me. It was a typical gabled attic with beams in the ceiling. The walls were roughly whitewashed and an old beige carpet covered the floor. Spring sunshine flooded in through a huge window in the sloping roof onto a large wooden table with a chair and an old battered Anglepoise lamp. An old sofa stood to one side, with faded cushions on it. All was bare and clean.

I felt almost sacrilegious opening the cupboard door. On one shelf there was a wooden box containing pencils, rulers, erasers and a collection of small pots containing

136

dried-up gouache. Next to that was a large heap of drawing paper, all A3 size. The actual drawings were in those huge artists' portfolios with tie fastenings that you see art-students struggling onto buses with. There were six of them, all full.

There were loads of sketches, many of them obviously of people met in the street: women with heavy shopping bags, kids playing on the pavements, people standing, bending, walking, running. There were backgrounds of varying sorts, some of which I recognized: the Abbaye de la Cambre, where I'd met Daniel; a row of gabled houses near the Gare Centrale; the fountains in the Square Ambiorix downtown. There were half-begun stories, none of them finished, the characters sketched in pencil, empty boxes where the words should have been. He had never found his voice, this young man. He had never had a story to tell.

But I was wrong. In the last portfolio of all, the one at the bottom of the pile, I found the answer to all my questions. There were still no words, but in the score or so beautifully drawn and coloured plates, the poor confused young man had told his own story, his and Marie-Paule's. The lines between reality and fantasy must have been blurred indeed.

They'd met by chance at someone else's exhibition, for which Marie-Paule's company had done the PR. It was, I suppose, love at first sight on both sides, by one of those unfathomable attractions of total opposites. They had fallen into bed immediately. Their erotic adventures were recorded in the most intimate, loving, beautifully depicted detail. I am not particularly naive, but I felt my ears growing hot as I turned the pages.

And then slowly had come the change; his growing panic about her fierce devotion. She wanted to make him famous. She offered money, connections, success, and the more she offered, the more frightened he became. She was taking him over, she wouldn't take no for an answer,

137

she wanted to own him, as she'd wanted to own every thing and person she'd ever loved. She'd never failed before. The last few pages were nightmarish in execution: the dark, rainswept night, the lights glistening on the railway lines, and the monolithic shape of the train as it bore down on him out of the darkness. He had drawn his own death and then gone out and made it come true. Except that it had been foggy that night, not rainy. But the result had been the same.

I closed the portfolio, cold, shaken with pity for the two of them. I understood Marie-Paule now. He must have been the only man she'd ever loved like that. The realization that she was pregnant must have come soon after the young man's death. There was no sign in the story that he had known. And she had directed her ferocious will-power to the sole end of making life easy for her child, snatched like an afterthought from the ruins of the passion. I sat back, awed anew by a personality that had derailed so many people's lives.

I left the studio as I'd found it and made my silent way downstairs. Madame Raczkowska was sitting at the table, the two pictures of her son and grandson in front of her. She'd been crying, but she was quiet now. She looked at me without attempting to hide her emotion. I sat down. I'd have liked to offer some gesture of physical comfort, but her dignity forbade it. I was reminded, oddly, of Agnès Gheyssens.

'I have been thinking,' she said. 'Perhaps it would be better to say nothing. There is no proof and too many people's lives will be upset.'

'I promised Daniel the truth. Now I've found out what it is, I can't just turn my back on it.'

'The truth can be very uncomfortable. Too uncomfortable.'

'For whom?'

'The grandparents. They will be upset. Maybe they will not let me see him. After all, why should they?'

'Common decency,' I replied. 'Agnès Gheyssens is a good woman. And don't you see that Daniel has to know? Everybody else has conspired to keep him in the dark. I'm damned if I'll do the same. It's just not fair.'

'You are very determined,' she said, with a slight flicker of a smile. 'I wish I had your confidence.'

I left soon after that, feeling rather exhausted, and went home. After lunch I sat down with Hortense on my lap and tried to think, but there are times when the grey cells simply announce they've had enough, and this was one. Somehow the thoughts slipped through my head and vanished, and the only reality left was Hortense's enthusiastic tramping as she tried to unpick my pullover with her claws.

Chapter Nineteen

I wondered briefly, as I set off for the Gheyssens house the next morning, what kind of bombshell I was about to set off.

I'd anticipated a fight with the maid, but I needn't have worried. As I drove up the street, I saw a bustle outside Agnès' front door. A large removal van was parked there, with men going in and out of the wide-open house carrying furniture and large cardboard boxes. So the Gheyssens were leaving town? I parked the car and strolled up. Nobody took much notice. I went up the steps and into the hall. I could hear voices upstairs, together with faint bumps and crashes. The hall furniture had gone already and the carpet was up, leaving a light rectangle on the parquet floor. Half a dozen boxes were stacked in one corner, together with a couple of standard lamps with their electric flexes wound round their stems and lampshades at their feet. It was all very dusty.

A door stood open into a small *vestiaire*; I could see a row of coat-hooks with garments still hanging on them, and an umbrella-stand with a few handles poking out of it. I wandered over to have a closer look. Crashing and bumping heralded the appearance of four large sweaty men manoeuvring a sofa bed down the stairs, with much under-the-breath swearing and grunting. They disappeared out of the door and I heard shouts and more bumps from outside, but I didn't pay much attention. I was too busy staring at the contents of the *vestiaire*.

I turned and leaned against the wall, finding it difficult to breathe, and Agnès came down the stairs and saw me. She stopped as if she'd been hit in the face, eyes wide. She'd aged about ten years since I'd last seen her a couple of days ago.

We stared at one another in silence. Then she seemed to recover herself. She came down the last few stairs, gripping the rail tightly, and said, in a voice that only trembled a little bit, 'Daniel isn't here. He's gone to our house at the coast.'

My own voice crossed hers on the last word. 'With your husband?'

She seemed to shrink, but her dignity stayed with her. 'Yes,' she said.

'Do you think he'll be safe?' I enquired.

She whispered, 'What do you mean?' but she knew what I meant all right. Her eyes looked sick.

'It was your husband who beat me up, wasn't it?' I said, hardily. I should have felt sorry for her, but I only felt anger. 'The incorruptible Pierre Gheyssens. Wearing that coat in there and carrying that stick. I expect those nice shoes are around here somewhere too.'

At the back of my mind I suddenly realized what had clinched the discovery: the same reason why I'd been so sure it had been a man who attacked me and not a woman: the faint but recognizable sweet scent of pipe tobacco which hung about that coat.

Agnès clung to the stair-rail, her face white and shrivelled, and suddenly, the explosion of anger was out of me and I felt a flood of pity for her. I ran across the hall and up the stairs and caught her arm.

'Sit down,' I said. 'You'll fall. It was him, wasn't it?'

Crouched on the stairs, she looked up at me and whispered, 'Yes. He came in very late the night you were attacked, looking so angry. I didn't know then, but when I saw your face on Thursday, I – I suspected. You see – it's happened before.'

The removal men came back in and clumped in a silent body up the stairs, casting curious glances at the lady of the house and me and leaving a strong whiff of sweat behind them.

'My husband has always been a very – impatient man,' Agnès said falteringly. 'He was an only son – his father died early, so he was head of the family from a very young age. He had to take the responsibility for his mother and sisters, make all the decisions. Don't you see? He has to be in charge. He can't stand being opposed. It makes him furious. Violent.' Her voice dropped almost to a whisper. 'You understand.'

I understood. Her hands were trembling. I took them gently in mine and said, 'Haven't you ever told anyone?'

She shook her head. 'It began as soon as we were married. He'd just joined the police and things were very difficult for us. I married straight out of school and didn't know anything. I went to my mother once and tried to tell her, but she said it must be my own fault – I must be doing something wrong. And there was no one else I could go to. It's been going on for years.'

She smiled, a sad, desperate smile. 'I tried to do what my mother told me. I learned to recognize the signs and keep out of the way, not to provoke him. But since he retired, he's been impossible: angry, bad-tempered, completely unreasonable. Nothing mattered to him except his career. And Marie-Paule, of course. Someone from the police told him those terrible things you found out about her. He got into such a rage I was afraid he'd have a stroke. So when I saw the bruises on your face the other day, I guessed what had happened. I'm so, so sorry.'

'You've got to tell Roland,' I said. 'For all our sakes. You've got to.'

'How can I? Pierre's my husband. I can't give him up to the police. There's his reputation to think of, his whole career. What will our friends say – and the family?'

'He needs help,' I said. 'He's already beaten me up and

142

you say he's been abusing you for years. God knows what else he's liable to do. Don't you see that Daniel might be in danger? You've got to put an end to this. Dear Heaven, Agnès, you've got to tell the truth.'

'I know,' she said wretchedly. 'I know. I've been thinking about it for hours and hours, going over and over it in my mind, and I know you're right.'

The men came back down the stairs, puffing under a mahogany dressing-table with a marble top. We had to move. I took Agnès' arm and helped her get up from the stairs.

'I'm sorry, there's nowhere to sit,' she said, in a more normal voice. 'You came at a bad time.' And then the conventional phrase must have struck her as ludicrously inappropriate, because she gave a short, unhappy laugh, almost like a sob.

'I was lucky to catch you,' I said. 'I only came to give you some news about Daniel. I've found out who his father is.'

'Oh,' she said. Then, with an effort, 'Is he alive?'

'No, he died ten years ago,' I told her and saw, despite herself, weary relief in her face. 'He was a young Polish artist called Jerzy Raczkowski. His mother's still alive, though. I think she'll want to meet Daniel – and you.'

'She won't want to – take him away, will she?'

'I think she's more concerned that *you* will,' I said wryly. 'You'll have to talk it out with her.'

'Yes,' she said. 'Afterwards.' She looked me straight in the face then, and said, 'I know you feel you had to find out the truth, but do you know what you've done? You've destroyed my family.'

I shouldn't have got angry, she didn't deserve it, but I'm only human.

'Listen,' I said, 'I'm not blaming you, but if your family had been more honest right from the start, none of this would have happened. Marie-Paule lied and cheated and manipulated, and you and your husband went along with

143

it, no matter what the cost to everybody else involved. OK, so they're all grown-up people and can look after themselves. Maybe. But Daniel's another matter. None of you had any right to cheat him out of the truth.'

'You're so sure of yourself,' she said. 'I wish I were.'

It was the second time in several days that someone had made that remark. Maybe it was true.

Agnès sighed. 'I suppose I should make that call,' she said.

I waited with her till the police arrived. Roland came in person and took Agnès' statement in the half-empty house, sitting in a chair that had been hurriedly unloaded from the removal van. He wasn't overjoyed to see me. He had a few more cutting things to say about amateurs meddling in police business, but I'd heard it all before. Afterwards he leaned back in his chair and surveyed me, half angry and half ironical.

'I suppose I ought to thank you for clearing up at least one element of this case,' he said with a wry mouth. 'But it doesn't actually help us much with the basic problem.'

'Have you found Consuela?' I asked. 'What did she say?'

He made a short noise rather like a snort.

'They can't find her,' he said. 'Her family don't know where she is. Or they say they don't. She and her sister have disappeared. Half the Spanish police force is out looking for them. If she was lying and she was at the scene of the crime just after one, then she's a prime suspect.'

'I just can't believe it,' I said, remembering the plain, uncomplicated face. 'Anyway, surely you can't arrest her on hearsay? You've got no proof.'

'We'll have to try and make her admit it,' Roland said. He sighed. 'If only we'd had a chance to question Lemaître. It's most likely, after all, that he killed Madame Vanderauwera.'

'He genuinely didn't seem to know she was dead and I

144

don't think he was lying,' I said. 'And he didn't have a motive, anyway. As he said, she was his best customer. And where's the weapon?'

For the first time, a glint of real humour showed in the colourless eyes. 'You should consider joining the police,' he observed.

I thought it wisest not to answer that. Instead I said, 'Are you going to let Luc go?'

'Not unless he accounts for where he was at the time of the murder. My nose tells me he's hiding something.'

Damn Luc. I'd persuaded Agnès to tell the truth about her husband, and here I was concealing facts for Luc's sake. I wondered if I should get my head read. Roland, meanwhile, was reading my face.

'Don't worry,' he said maliciously. 'We'll find out sooner or later.'

Chapter Twenty

There hadn't been much in the papers about the case up till then, thanks to Gheyssens' influence, but the new revelations were far too juicy for the press to pass up, so it was all there the next day. Daughter of highly placed ex-Police Chief murdered in love-nest, ex-policeman husband in jail, ex-mistress of husband attacked by father, battered wife story, with pictures, comment and all the salacious details. I got off relatively lightly: no picture and my name spelled wrong, as usual. Pierre Gheyssens was under psychiatric care by then, so he didn't see any of it, but poor Agnès must have been in agonies of guilt. She was the type.

None of us were prepared for the next development, however, least of all me. I was in the local paper-shop a couple of days later when the new edition of *Le Soir* arrived, all tied up in bundles, with the headline 'NEW ARREST EXPECTED IN GHEYSSENS CASE' and I'd hardly got home when the telephone started ringing.

Maggie. Again. In a state.

'Matilda, you've got to do something. Oh, this is absolutely ridiculous. Do you know what those idiots have done now? They've arrested Piet!'

'They've what?'

'They got an anonymous letter saying he'd done it and it turns out that a gun in his collection is the murder weapon, though I don't know how they can tell. I've had Lieve here all morning weeping all over me, and

146

everything's in an uproar. Can't you do something?'

'But what?' I protested, stupidly.

'You've got to come down and talk to Piet. He's absolutely distraught, you can imagine what this must be like for him. I don't know what the police are playing at. Matilda, please come and help.'

I couldn't get through to Commissaire Roland and the Brussels police refused to give me any details, so I got in the car and drove straight to Lier, reflecting somewhat wryly on Maggie's apparent faith in my infallibility.

Maggie's small house was popular today. There was a police car outside, and a little group of people with cameras and tape recorders: the local press, no doubt. As I elbowed past and charged up the path under the unwelcome pop of flashbulbs, the front door opened and Roland came out. We both stopped abruptly.

'Miss Haycastle, what a surprise!' he said, ironically.

'What's going on?' I demanded.

He sighed. 'Read the papers,' he said, and made to go past me. I grabbed his arm.

'Why've you arrested Piet? What possible motive could he have had?'

'I'm sure you'll want to ask him,' Roland replied.

'What about Luc? Are you going to hold him now?'

He turned and gave me one of his penetrating looks.

'That seems to matter a great deal to you, doesn't it? Enough maybe for you to send an anonymous note implicating someone else?'

I dropped his arm as if it were red-hot.

'You think I'd get Luc off the hook by implicating another member of his family? Well, thanks.'

'Somebody did,' he said. 'And we'd like to know who.'

'Analyse the writing.'

'It was done on a computer, with a laser-printer. You have a computer and printer at home, don't you? And access to one at work?'

'So do millions of other people,' I said. This is an unexpected aspect of progress. Gone are the days when you could identify anonymous typed notes by the chipped 'c' and the weak 'w'.

Roland gave me an old-fashioned look and set off down the path.

'What about fingerprints?' I asked, after his retreating back.

'Miss Haycastle, go home,' he said over his shoulder. I watched him get into the police car amid the flashing bulbs.

The entire Vanderauwera-Giestelinck family was inside Maggie's house, with the exception of Piet, who I supposed must still be at the police station. They were arranging bail and hoped he would be home soon. Everybody wanted to talk except Brigitte's parents, who sat side by side in a corner in silence. They had all the details I needed. Roland had received a letter, posted in Brussels, denouncing Piet as the killer and suggesting they look at his gun collection. They'd found a Browning of the right calibre; and forensic tests had shown it to be the gun that killed Marie-Paule. Piet's fingerprints were on the gun.

'What about the letter?' I asked.

'Half the post-office workers in Brussels seem to have handled the letter,' Maggie said bitterly. 'Not to mention half the idiots in the police station, so that's no use as a lead.'

'But why do they think Piet would have done it? What's his motive? He told me he hadn't seen Marie-Paule for years.'

There was an embarrassed silence, unusual for the Vanderauweras.

'OK,' I said, 'out with it.'

'He went to see her a couple of weeks before she died,' Katrien said, rather red-faced. 'She humiliated him and threw him out of the house.'

'But what did he want to see her about?' I asked, staring.

On the sofa, Tante Lieve raised a red, swollen face from her sopping hanky and wailed, 'I didn't know. He never said a thing.'

'He needed money,' Katrien said miserably. Her usual animation was noticeably missing. 'The Lotto money had run out. He'd spent it all.'

'And he thought Marie-Paule would lend him some?' I asked, incredulously.

'Well, after all,' Katrien said, 'she was family.'

'And she'd just had that inheritance from her aunt,' Brigitte added.

Hope springs eternal. Poor Piet. I could just imagine what Marie-Paule had said to him. She must have really enjoyed it.

'Does he have an alibi?' I asked. Another embarrassed silence filled the room.

'He says he was at the cinema,' Brigitte said.

'Does anyone remember seeing him there?'

'It was the sort of cinema where they make a point of not remembering the customers' faces,' Maggie said impatiently. 'In case they have to identify them later.'

This was worse and worse. I must say I hadn't envisaged Piet as one of the dirty mackintosh brigade, but you never can tell.

'I'll have to talk to him,' I said. 'Have you got any news of Luc?'

'We called Brussels,' Brigitte said. 'They're going to release Luc this afternoon.'

'And thank goodness for that,' Maggie said with a sigh.

Tante Lieve raised her wet face again, aggressively. 'It's all very well for you to say that, but what about my Piet? He doesn't deserve it, which is more than you can say for that son of yours.'

Maggie opened her mouth, but the family moved in well-drilled formation to avert confrontation and potential nastiness.

'Now, now,' Brigitte said briskly, moving in and putting an arm round Tante Lieve's shoulder, 'you know you don't really mean that. There's no need to worry. Matilda will do something about Piet, won't you, Matilda?'

They were all looking at me with hopeful eyes, but I was wondering glumly what on earth I was doing there.

I got to see Piet that afternoon, at his lawyer's house, where he'd taken refuge. He looked ill. His hands were trembling and he seemed to have lost weight. He was pathetically glad to see me.

'I had nothing to do with her death, I swear it,' he said. 'In spite of everything. I had nothing to do with it. I've never killed anything in my life, not even an ant. Not deliberately, anyway. You've got to believe me.'

'But you're a good shot?' I asked.

He nodded miserably. He was a crack shot; the family had told me about all the trophies he'd won.

'Could anybody have had access to the gun apart from you? Could it have gone missing for a couple of days without you noticing?'

'I suppose so. There were lots of people in the house during that week when Marie-Paule was killed. Mother had her charity committee, and then I had the lads from the shooting club, and there was a party for Brigitte's parents – their fortieth wedding anniversary or something. And the family are in and out all day.'

'Can you make a list of names?' I asked.

'I suppose so,' he said doubtfully.

'Do you have any idea who could have written that note? And why?'

'Not a clue,' he said helplessly, spreading his hands out. 'I don't have any enemies. Not as far as I know, anyway.'

'And your alibi?' I asked, and watched him blush a deep scarlet.

He wouldn't meet my eyes.

'You don't know what it's like,' he muttered. 'Looking like this. Girls aren't interested. They never have been. Nobody wants to go out with me. And now there isn't

150

even the money. I don't know what I'm going to do. I can't face going back to work.'

'Sell the guns,' I said. 'They must be worth a fair bit. And get a job doing something you like.'

'I just don't like working,' he said dolefully.

I'd have laughed, if it hadn't been so serious.

Back at Maggie's, the family was on the point of leaving at last. The bright light of day showed up all the lines of worry on Katrien's face as she helped her mother into the car. She looked much older suddenly, behind the big spectacles. All the bubble and squeak had gone.

'This is the worst thing that's happened since Dad died,' she said, a catch in her voice. 'Suppose Piet goes to prison?'

'We're not there yet,' I said. 'Try not to worry.'

They drove off, and Brigitte appeared, shepherding her parents down the path.

'We heard from Luc,' she called to me. 'He's out of custody.'

'Well, that's one good thing,' I answered. I watched her put the old people into the car, with her usual patience and competence. As she straightened up, she said to me, 'I know you'll be able to help Piet. I've got every confidence in you.'

'I'm glad someone has,' I said, rather wryly.

'I was wondering if you'd be free to have lunch next week,' Brigitte went on. 'I'm coming to Brussels again – another appointment with my doctor – but I thought we could meet, if you'd like to.'

'Yes, of course,' I said, though without much enthusiasm, I have to admit. 'Give me a call and we'll arrange a time and place.'

She seemed pleased by that, to my relief.

I was feeling tired. I plodded up the path and went in. Maggie was at the sideboard, pouring out sherry.

'I couldn't very well say it with Lieve here,' she said,

handing me a glass, 'but at least we can celebrate Luc's release. Did Brigitte tell you?'

'Yes,' I said, collapsing into an armchair and stretching out my legs. 'Is he coming here?'

'No,' Maggie said, rather abruptly. I peered at her and she said, rather too hastily, 'I expect he wants to be on his own for a while. It's quite understandable.'

There was a short silence. It didn't feel much like a celebration.

'Who is this doctor of Brigitte's, anyway?' I asked, to change the subject. 'He doesn't seem to be doing much good, if she keeps having to go back.'

'She's having a course of treatment,' Maggie explained. 'And the doctor's very good. It's a woman, by the way. I've been going to her for years, and I recommended her to Brigitte. I don't know about you, but I'd rather see a woman gynaecologist than a man.'

She rabbited on about gynaecologists for a while, but I was only listening with half an ear. I was thinking that whoever sent that note knew the gun was the murder weapon. And that meant that whoever sent that note might well be the murderer.

Chapter Twenty-One

Marius came to dinner the next evening. I was rather in two minds about it. I liked Marius and enjoyed his company, but I was half-dreading some sort of declaration of intent; and dinner between two unattached adults of different sexes, no matter what anybody says to the contrary, always has a slight scent of seduction about it. I even thought about cancelling, but finally decided it would be chicken.

I made a point of not getting out the glad rags and the warpaint, but it didn't seem to make much difference; the usual appreciative look was in Marius' eyes when he came in. He, on the other hand, had made a special effort and looked positively debonair. He handed over a rather decent bottle of wine and a bunch of flowers, and chucked Hortense under the chin.

'What news?' he said.

I filled him in while we were eating. It took a while. He frowned with concentration, listening. He'd read all about Piet's arrest in the papers, but I was able to tell him what had really happened. And, of course, the news about Daniel's father.

'Congratulations,' he said warmly. 'Your hard work finally paid off. What was Daniel's reaction?'

'I haven't seen him yet. Agnès packed him off to the coast before I could tell him, and things have been so upside-down since, there hasn't been a chance. We arranged that I'd go out there and talk to him when everything's quietened down.'

'And Vanderauwera's out of prison?'

He always referred to Luc by his surname. It was funny the instant dislike they'd taken to one another.

'So it seems. He hasn't been in touch. I don't expect him to be.'

'And he never did manage to provide an alibi?'

'No,' I said. I could feel myself reddening slightly and hoped Marius put it down to the wine. 'But once Piet was arrested, they couldn't go on holding Luc as well. I said he had a clever lawyer.'

'And knew all the angles,' Marius said ironically. 'And now his family expects you to prove Piet's innocence too?'

'Everybody thinks I'm an expert,' I said. 'But honestly, I haven't a clue where to start. There aren't any leads at all. Consuela's disappeared and Christian's dead.'

'Go back to Marie-Paule's own life,' Marius advised. 'Find out what she was doing just before her death. There must be some clue.'

'She had her hair done and she went to the doctor.'

'Go and talk to the hairdresser and the doctor. Have you got their names?'

'I wrote them down,' I said, getting up and going to my handbag. The names were in my diary. Coiffure Rosalie and Doctor Goldstein.

'I'll get onto it first thing,' I said.

I went into the kitchen to unpackage the dessert, and the phone rang.

'Blast,' I said, struggling with the ice-cream cake. 'Answer it, Marius, would you?'

A moment later, he appeared in the kitchen doorway, looking solemn.

'It's Vanderauwera,' he said.

It bloody well would be.

I grabbed the phone and snapped 'Yes,' conscious of extreme irritation and not a little embarrassment.

154

'I just wanted to let you know I'm out,' Luc's voice said. 'And to say thanks for keeping quiet.'

'That's all right,' I answered. 'Are you OK? What was it like?'

'Interesting,' Luc said, with the ghost of a grim chuckle. 'I wouldn't like to repeat the experience, though. Matilda, will you do something for me?'

So that was it. 'Yes,' I said, without enthusiasm.

'Maggie says you've found out who Daniel's real father is. When you see Daniel next, just tell him if he ever needs anything, he can count on me.'

'Why don't you tell him yourself?' I asked. There seemed to be a listening silence from the living-room. There was a silence on the other end of the phone too.

'Because I can't face it,' Luc said, finally. 'Just tell him, will you?'

'I'll tell him,' I said.

When I went back into the living-room, Marius wasn't there. He was in the kitchen, sorting out the ice-cream cake I'd abandoned. A discreet man.

'Sorry,' I said.

'Not your fault,' he answered, picking up the dish. 'You didn't know he was going to call. This looks delicious.'

Hortense had taken advantage of our absence to jump on the table and start hoovering up the crumbs. I shooshed her off and we sat down again.

'He only wanted me to pass on a message to Daniel,' I said.

'Can't he do it himself?' Marius asked sharply.

'That's what I asked him,' I replied with a laugh.

After a moment, Marius said, 'I'm sorry. I was out of line. What you do is your business and you don't have to explain.'

The ice-cream cake was melting round the edges.

'Matilda,' Marius said, a serious look on his face, 'there's something I've got to tell you.'

155

Oh dear, here it was then. I steeled myself, and waited.

'I'm going away,' Marius said. 'I took your advice and signed up with *Médecins Sans Frontières.* I'm off to Afghanistan in two weeks' time.'

I was really going to have to be careful about giving people advice. I stared wordlessly at Marius, completely taken by surprise.

'It's the best thing,' he said gently. 'You know how dissatisfied I am with what I'm doing here. And there's nothing really to keep me here, is there?'

And there wasn't. I'd hoped to find a friend and I had, but for him, I suppose, friendship wasn't quite enough. And he was old enough and wise enough to know that I couldn't give him what he wanted. Not just now, anyway. I swallowed and found my voice, conscious of a real sense of disappointment.

'I hope you'll be very happy,' I said, and I'm glad to say I meant it.

'I'm sure I will be,' Marius said, starting to eat his ice-cream. 'There are one or two details still to be sorted out. For example, the house. I'll be putting it up for rent, but something Yasmina said made me think you might like to have first refusal. How about it? I'll be a very reasonable landlord.'

'But I haven't even thought about moving!' I exclaimed, glancing round the apartment. But I had to admit, the idea settled in my imagination, took root and blossomed with no encouragement at all. A house! A garden!

'Think it over for a couple of days and let me know,' Marius said. 'I won't do anything till I hear from you.' He paused and said, 'I'd like to think of you living in my house. We can negotiate the rent. You'd have to look after the plants. And Yasmina goes with the deal, needless to say.'

I thought about it after he'd gone, while I was doing the washing-up. Hortense, having done her usual efficient pre-wash of the plates, was sitting on the kitchen table cleaning her paws. I couldn't come to a conclusion, so I suspended the debate and sat down to finish up the bottle of wine, for Marius was a moderate drinker.

'Afghanistan,' I said to Hortense, who took no notice. Then I said, 'Oh well, it probably wouldn't have worked anyway.' Then I said, 'In any case, I could hardly expect him to wait around till I felt like it again, could I?'

Hortense stopped washing, considered me for a moment with alien golden eyes, and then obviously decided I needed distracting, for she stepped down delicately from the table onto my lap and turned round a couple of times before settling. The warm solid weight was comforting. Cats are a good antidote to self-pity.

Chapter Twenty-Two

I checked out the *salon de coiffure* the next morning. It was a high-class establishment on the Avenue Louise. I got a few funny looks when I asked for the person who used to cut Marie-Paule's hair; they obviously thought I was a thrill-seeking ghoul. You meet all sorts in the hairdressing business. However, the rather colourful, chatty young man who bustled over swallowed my story about being a reporter and became positively garrulous at the sight of a thousand-franc note. The only trouble was, he couldn't cast any light on the matter. Marie-Paule had been one of those clients who never talked, which must have been a sore trial for him. Also she'd been a real tight-wad: never tipped. Tight as a mouse's rear-end, he said cheerfully. I didn't get the impression she'd been his favourite customer. He asked me if I'd ever considered going auburn. I looked thoughtfully at his own blue and green love-locks and left before he could start advising me about my split ends.

I hoped I'd get on better at the doctor's.

'You ought to think about coming off the pill at your age,' said Doctor Goldstein, *Gynécologie et Obstétrie*.

Doctors always tell you things you don't want to hear. I'd been having the odd second thought about the pill for a couple of years now but so far had managed to postpone making a decision about it.

'If you're not married and have no steady relationship

at present,' the doctor continued briskly, 'there seems little point stuffing yourself with chemicals for no reason. I'm not saying there's any immediate danger. You're very healthy and you don't smoke, so you've got a couple of years to think about it. But mechanical methods are very reliable these days, and they do present other advantages. Though if you've really made up your mind not to have children, you might as well have your tubes tied. Or are you hanging on, hoping?'

'Certainly not,' I said. Motherhood has never appealed to me, and certainly not now, at my advanced age.

Doctor Goldstein was small, dark and efficient. Her office was modern and uncluttered, with sunlight streaming brightly through white net curtains. I could hear the voices of children playing outside in the street.

'Very wise,' she said. 'Too many women leave it till the last minute and then wonder why they have so many complications. Nature seems to have intended peak childbearing time to be around the age of seventeen, so you're pushing your luck after thirty-five.'

'It's Catch-22,' I said with a laugh. 'There are too many other things to do when you're young: travel, have fun, build up a career. You can't do that so easily with kids.'

'You can't do it at all, not without something suffering. Motherhood's a twenty-four hour job, and it goes on for years. If you want fun or a career, you shouldn't have kids.'

'Have you got children?' I asked curiously.

She smiled rather ruefully. 'Two,' she said. 'I'm lucky – I had the career too. But fun's been in rather short supply.'

'Do you regret it?'

'Sometimes. But you have to make your choices and stand by them.'

I'd made a regular appointment with Doctor Goldstein and at least had the satisfaction of knowing that I was in good working order. Now for the difficult part.

'I have a confession to make,' I said.

159

The doctor raised dark eyebrows.

'I made this appointment because I needed to ask you a few questions about Marie-Paule Vanderauwera.'

'You mean Gheyssens? She used her maiden name. Are you a reporter?' Doctor Goldstein asked abruptly, frowning.

'No. I'm a friend of the family. You know that her husband was arrested at first and now they've decided it was a cousin who did it?'

'Yes. I read it in the papers. The police seem to be making their usual hash of things.'

'Madame Vanderauwera's mother-in-law has asked me to make a few private enquiries and I know Marie-Paule had an appointment with you the week before she died. I just wondered if you could give me any clues as to her state of mind.'

'I couldn't possibly give you any medical details,' Doctor Goldstein said, still frowning. 'It's confidential.'

'I understand that. I'm more interested in your impressions. Did you know her well?'

'Madame Gheyssens had been coming to me for a number of years, but I can't say I knew her well. She wasn't a forthcoming kind of woman.'

'No,' I said. 'Was this a routine appointment?'

'Perfectly routine. She was in the habit of consulting me every six months or so.'

'And she didn't say or do anything unusual?'

'Not as far as I remember. It was a Wednesday, wasn't it? Early in March?'

'I think so,' I said.

'Let's have a look.' She reached for her appointment book and flipped the pages back. 'Wednesday, March the third at eleven a.m.'

'Can I look?' I asked and she handed the book over.

Doctor Goldstein was obviously popular. Every day was filled with consultations. Next to the hour of eleven was written, 'Gheyssens-Vanderauwera'.

160

And suddenly, staring at that closely written page, I experienced a revelation. I went hot and cold, red and white. Doctor Goldstein said curiously, 'What is it?'

I'd forgotten she was there. I stared at her blindly, then said, 'Nothing. Nothing at all. I'd better be going.'

I paid the consultation fee, thanked Doctor Goldstein for her help, and left. The only way out was through the waiting-room, which was tiny, with four chairs in it. I knew now how St Paul had felt on the road to Damascus.

I had to get home and think. It was warm in the apartment, and I opened the windows; the sunlight streaming through the panes showed up the winter's dirt on them. It was quiet. Somewhere in the street, somebody was playing a piano, not too badly at all. The sound floated gently in and I listened, trying to get my thoughts in order. Hortense was nowhere to be seen; probably fast asleep in the laundry basket, as usual at this time of the day.

I now knew who'd killed Marie-Paule. What I didn't know was why. And there was one more piece of information to check out before I did anything. I reached for the phone to call Maggie.

The doorbell rang.

Not the bell downstairs, but the apartment door. The *concierge*, probably – anyone else would ring downstairs. I put the receiver down and went to the door.

It was Brigitte Giestelinck.

Chapter Twenty-Three

In one hand she had a carrier bag from the most exclusive delicatessen in town, and in the other a flat *pâtisserie* box dangling from a string. She was smiling. She was the last person in the universe I wanted to see. I stood gaping, and she laughed and said, 'Hello, Matilda. I thought it might be a good day to have lunch. I've brought all the stuff. May I come in?'

She walked in while I was still trying to think of an answer, looked round and smiled again.

'What a lovely apartment. It's just the way I imagined it. I always thought you and I'd have the same tastes. Can I look round?'

It was too late to make an excuse now. I closed the front door and said grimly, 'Be my guest. Let me have your coat. What did you bring?'

'Some pâté and salads, and an apricot tart,' she said, handing me the parcels and struggling out of her dark-blue coat. 'I know I'm being nosey but do you mind if I look in the bedroom?'

'Go ahead. I'll be in the kitchen.'

Wondering how I was going to handle this, I set about laying the table, and opened a bottle of wine. I felt I needed a drink. I'd just finished taking the lids off the little plastic tubs of salad when she came back in, still smiling.

'It's beautiful. I've always wanted a place like this, but I couldn't really leave my parents on their own, not at their age. It wouldn't be fair.'

'I suppose not,' I said. 'Sit down, Brigitte. This looks delicious. Glass of wine?'

'Please. I've been wanting to have a chat with you for a long time – I mean, just the two of us.'

'What about?' I asked cautiously and she said, 'Luc,' and laughed at my expression of surprise.

'Don't worry. I haven't come to take him away from you. I'm really glad you're so happy together. I hope you don't mind me saying this, but I like to think of you as my sister. We're very alike in many ways. Especially the way we feel about Luc.'

Maggie must have kept her mouth shut about my split with Luc.

Brigitte helped herself to pâté, automatically putting a helping on my plate too. The perfect nurse.

'Luc and I were very close as children,' she said. 'Living in the same town, of course, we were bound to see a lot of each other. But after his father died, he went off to school in England and I only saw him in the holidays. And as we got older, we followed different paths and careers. The usual story with childhood sweethearts. He did his military service and joined the gendarmerie and I was training as a nurse, so it was inevitable we'd drift apart. But I never stopped loving him. I used to live for the moments we could be together. To be honest, there wasn't very much else in my life at all. I was sure he'd finally come and settle down in Lier again, once he'd sown his wild oats. But then he went and married Marie-Paule.'

It had the ring of the most banal *roman à l'eau de rose*, repeated so often inside Brigitte's head that it had become reality. I felt a terrible pity; Luc had never given this woman more than the most cursory thought and she'd built up a whole love story round him. I was going to have to be careful where I put my feet. Not in my mouth, if possible.

'The marriage must have come as a terrible shock,' I

said carefully, watching her face. There was no change of expression. She was quite matter-of-fact.

'Well, of course it did. To the whole family. Anyone could see what kind of woman she was – any other woman, that is. The men were all blind. I tried to warn Luc, but he wouldn't listen to me. And then, when Daniel was born, we all knew what had happened. Poor Luc had no idea what he was getting himself into.'

'Weren't you jealous?' I asked, helping myself to some *champignons à la grecque* which I didn't want. 'I know I would have been.'

She didn't reply immediately. I glanced quickly up, but her face was still serene. 'A little. But you see, I'd really given up hope by that time. One has to be realistic. Our love could never have been what it was. I was older, he was older, there were my parents to think of. You know how it is.'

'Yes,' I said. 'People drift apart.'

'But everything's all right now,' Brigitte said, smiling radiantly. 'He's with you. You're nothing like Marie-Paule. I really like you. I hope we're going to be close friends.'

I'm no psychologist, but the chilling thought flashed through my mind that through me, she was really hoping to stay close to Luc. I wondered briefly what she'd do if I told her we'd separated.

'I only met Marie-Paule once,' I said, 'but she didn't exactly strike me as a pleasant person. It must have been difficult for you, seeing them at family gatherings and so on.'

Brigitte finished her pâté and put down her knife and fork. 'Not really,' she said. 'She didn't bother much with Lier and I don't come up to Brussels very often. As I told you before, I hadn't seen her for years.'

'Strange,' I said. 'Considering you and she and Maggie all share the same gynaecologist, it's amazing you never met there.'

164

'Yes, it is, isn't it?' Brigitte wiped her lips with her paper napkin. 'But I suppose Doctor Goldstein's got scores of patients.'

'What about Wednesday 3rd March?' I said. 'At eleven-twenty?'

Brigitte became quite still, her wide-open eyes fixed on my face.

'Marie-Paule had the eleven o'clock appointment,' I said. 'You must have been in the waiting room when she came out, and she had to pass you to leave the office. You must have seen her and she must have seen you. I'm sure Doctor Goldstein could confirm it.'

I'd known that ever since I'd seen the name under Marie-Paule's in the doctor's appointment book. The name 'Giestelinck, B.'.

Brigitte gave a quick nervous laugh. 'You are clever,' she said. 'I'd completely forgotten. I've been there so many times in the past few months. Yes, now you come to mention it, I did see her there.'

I'd gone too far to turn back now. I moved the remains of the pâté off the table, then picked up the knife and cut a slice of apricot tart, which I pushed over to my guest. My hands were shaking slightly.

'Did she say anything?' I asked. 'Knowing her, I'll bet she said something nasty. She wouldn't have missed an opportunity like that.'

This was a random guess, but it turned out to be bang on the nose. Maybe I was a psychologist after all. There was a long, long silence, while Brigitte's face slowly darkened, as if with remembered anger.

'She stopped and looked at me,' she said softly. 'She looked me up and down in that deliberate contemptuous way she had. She had a turquoise dress on and a long fur coat, a beautiful, soft, grey fur coat. One of her lovers must have bought it for her. I'd never be able to afford a coat like that. She sneered and said, "Why, it's Luc's little lamb." That's what she used to call me. Luc's little lamb.

165

Always following him about. Oh, I hated her for that.'

This was where things might get sticky. But I was sure of my guess now.

'You hated her,' I said quietly, 'and you loved Luc. You killed her, didn't you? You were one of the people who had access to Piet's gun collection. You were in and out of the house; there was a party for your parents there that week. You took the gun and went back to Brussels. You got to the house just as Christian Lemaître was leaving. He saw a middle-aged woman in a dark-blue coat walking down the street and he thought it was the maid, but it was you. Marie-Paule was alone, so she must have opened the door herself. You went in and shot her.'

After all, one plain middle-aged woman in a dark-blue coat looks much like any other to the casual observer.

'You were very lucky,' I said. 'Nobody saw you, or heard the shot. You let yourself out, went home and replaced the gun without anyone noticing it had gone. But when you heard Luc had been arrested, you had to do something to take the suspicion off him. So you sent the police an anonymous note, implicating Piet.'

There was no movement from the woman across the table. I said, 'You can't let Piet be tried for something he didn't do. You must go to the police and tell the truth. I'll go with you, if you like.'

She looked up then. Luckily, her expression gave me a micro-second's warning. As I flung myself desperately backwards, Brigitte exploded from her chair, snatched up the knife I'd used to cut the apricot tart, and blundered madly forward into the kitchen table, so beside herself that she was scarcely aware it was there. I found myself jammed up against the gas-cooker, my chair knocked sideways, with Brigitte making wild stabs and swipes at me across the width of the table. She hadn't the faintest idea how to use a knife – she held it like a heroine in a melodrama. Her eyes were staring, her face suddenly scarlet. Her breath was coming in huge, painful gasps, like a sick animal's.

166

She wasn't tall, but she was a solid woman and my frail kitchen table was all that stood between us. I thrust at it with all my strength, sending Brigitte staggering back, then reached wildly behind me and grabbed the first thing I could find to throw at her. It was a Teflon soup ladle – she made a bear-like batting motion at it with her free hand and it fell harmlessly to the floor. I followed it up with wooden spoons, egg-whisks, potato-peelers and tea-strainers, which she fended off in a mad whirl like a demented juggler. It was perfectly ludicrous – my breath was coming in sobs too, but I wasn't sure they weren't crazy laughter. And then I scored – a cheese-grater caught her a glancing blow on the forehead and I saw a line of scarlet appear on her pale skin. She backed off, grunting, and raised a hand to her head. She was between me and the kitchen door – I couldn't make a dash for it.

She stared at the blood on her hand, then looked up at me with such wild hatred that I quailed. Striding forward, she seized the edge of the kitchen table and pushed it skittering aside. I was out of ammunition. Desperately, I seized up my fallen chair and brandished it at her, like a lion-tamer. For a second we faced one another.

And at that very moment, Hortense suddenly materialized on the table in that startling silent way cats have. She must have been wakened by the noise, and then caught the intriguing scent of pâté. Neither of us had heard or seen her approach. She was just suddenly there.

To my utter amazement, Brigitte gave a hoarse cry, dropped the knife and blundered back against the kitchen door, mouth opening and shutting in terror, eyes fixed on Hortense, who was sniffing at the remains of the apricot tart. Into my shocked brain came something Maggie had said. A phobia about dirt, insects and small animals! I couldn't move. I could only watch, frozen ludicrously in position, my chair still in my hands.

167

Disappointed, Hortense leapt down from the table, paused, and then advanced inquisitively towards Brigitte, tail up. A gobbling sound came out of Brigitte's open mouth. Clumsy and lumbering in her panic, she backed out through the kitchen door and ran heavily through the flat, her feet thudding. I heard the front door open and slam close. Then it was quiet.

Slowly, painfully, I lowered the chair to the ground. Hortense leapt on the draining-board, found the remains of the pâté, and settled down for a good tuck-in. You never know where the next meal's coming from.

Chapter Twenty-Four

The police picked Brigitte up with no trouble. She was wandering around without her coat and handbag, both of which she'd left in my flat, and she gave them no trouble. She wouldn't say anything at first, but then a neighbour of Marie-Paule's remembered seeing her in the street around lunch-time on the day of the murder, and faced with that she told them the whole story.

They dropped the charges against Piet immediately. He was extremely shaken by his brief experience of police custody. He'd lost several kilos, but set about putting them back on straight away. There was a small celebration lunch in Lier, to which I was invited. I went reluctantly, half-afraid that Luc might be there, but he wasn't.

'He's gone to Los Angeles,' Maggie told me, as we waited in the restaurant, cocktails in hand, for the final guest to arrive. 'A friend there offered him a job. I don't know how he's going to get a work permit, but I suppose there's always a way if you know the right people, isn't there?' After a moment she added, rather desolately, 'It's awfully far away.'

'Matilda!' Piet rolled massively over to us and waved to a waiter, who came quickly across with a fresh tray of *cocktails maison*. 'I've done what you suggested. I've sold the guns. They raised quite a bit – more than I expected, so I'm putting off looking for a job for a while. Till the end of summer, anyway. I thought you'd like to

169

know. Ah, I think I hear Katrien arriving at last. Now we can eat.'

'Typical!' Maggie said, as he moved ponderously off. 'If I were Lieve, I'd—'

'Throw him out,' I finished. 'How? You'd need a block and tackle. Anyway, she loves looking after him, any idiot can see that. Nobody seems very much upset about Brigitte, do they?'

'Well, she's not a Vanderauwera, she's a Giestelinck,' Maggie said cynically. I thought that Luc's departure must have upset her a great deal. 'And she's in good hands; it's not as if she'll go to prison. I'd give her a medal myself.'

'How are her parents taking it all?'

'I hate to say it, but they've got a new lease of life,' Maggie said, shaking her head. 'Trotting about all over the place. They're off to the Ardennes next weekend, for the first time in fifteen years. Still, I suppose they're not all that old. They must be about my age.'

I smiled but made no comment. The cocktails were champagne with peach liqueur, and the meal promised to be a long one. It was a nice restaurant. It belonged to a Vanderauwera brother-in-law; Belgians believe in keeping things in the family.

A babble of high-pitched noise announced Katrien's arrival. She kissed everyone enthusiastically and said, 'Have you heard? Olivier and Sabine are back together. Just imagine her taking him back after all that! I couldn't do it. Could you, Matilda?'

I didn't even try to reply, which was just as well, because Katrien went on immediately, 'Is it true you're moving? I'm sure Maggie said you were. How exciting. Are you going to another flat?'

She actually stopped to let me answer this time, so I did. 'No, a house. I don't know how Hortense is going to react, but I'm certainly looking forward to it.'

I couldn't have stayed in that flat, not after everything

170

that had happened. I wanted a clean start. So I'd accepted Marius' offer, which seemed to please him ridiculously. He'd left for Afghanistan the previous day. I hate saying goodbye.

'If there's anything we can do to help with the move, just let us know,' Katrien beamed, pushing her glasses up her nose. 'After all, you're family now. Well, come on, Piet, let's eat. What are we waiting for?'

As we filed into the dining room, I reflected wryly that Luc might have gone, but I, who have little or no family feeling, seemed somehow to have inherited all his relatives. I was slightly surprised to discover that I didn't mind.

I thought that again at the weekend, after an exhausting romp along the beach at Knokke with Daniel and Daisy. It was one of those clear blue days, filled with the bright light so beloved of the impressionist painters, but the wind was still sharp, so we found somewhere sheltered to sit and I gave Daniel Luc's last message.

'How can he do anything for me if he's in America?' Daniel asked, practically. 'It's too far away.'

'I think he meant it for later,' I said carefully.

Daniel thought for a minute. Then he said, 'Well, it doesn't really matter, if he's not my real father. I'm going to meet my grandmother next week. My other grandmother, I mean. And she's going to tell me all about my real father.'

I had to hand it to Agnès. There was a heroic streak in her. Or maybe it was just a strong sense of what was right. She had gone to see Madame Raczkowska, and I suppose had discovered that there was no threat in that passive, kind personality. After all, they both had the same thing in mind: Daniel's happiness. I glanced at the lively little face beside me; he was looking eagerly at the gay sails of the wind-surfers, who were having a hard time today because of the breeze. He seemed

171

remarkably untouched by everything that had happened. In his own way, he was as strong a personality as his mother had been. He'd be all right now. The way was clear in front of him, as clear as I could make it, anyhow.

'I'll race you to the pier,' I said.